Recklessly YOURS

AJ RANNEY

Rudy House Publishing

Recklessly Yours

Half Moon Lake Book 4

Developmental Edit by Michelle Fewer

Line, Copy, Proofreading by Beth Lawton at VB Edits

Cover by K.B. Barrett Designs

ISBN: 978-1-965124-01-7 (ebook)

ISBN: 978-1-965124-09-3 (paperback)

❀ Created with Vellum

To anyone who has ever struggled to be seen
or heard in a crowded room.
This one's for you.

Listen on Spotify!

Pretty Little Poison - Warren Zeiders
Shake It Off - Taylor Swift
Just A Kiss - Lady A
Nobody But You - Blake Shelton, Gwen Stefani
What Ifs - Kane Brown, Lauren Alaina
Ultra Violet (Light My Way) - U2
Single Ladies (Put a Ring on It) - Beyoncé
Ain't No Love In Oklahoma - Luke Combs
Babylon - David Gray
Say The Word - Livingston
Handle On You - Parker McCollum
A Few Hearts Ago - Kylie Morgan

Chapter One

"THIS ONE MIGHT ACTUALLY BE A KEEPER."

I glanced up and found my sister Ashley standing in the doorway to my office, holding a large bouquet of white roses and blue flowers.

"Huh?" I tilted my head, confused about what she was talking about. It couldn't be her husband. We *all* knew she thought he was a keeper.

She plucked the crisp white card from the bouquet and read it out loud. "Hey, beautiful. Can't wait to see you again soon." Her face lit with a smile. "Who is he?" Before I could respond, she shook her head. "Don't tell me it's a guy from those dating sites you've been using."

Sighing, I sat back in my chair. *Here we go again.* The same tirade for the hundredth time. I'd let her say her piece, and then, if I was lucky, she would leave my office and let me get back to work.

"I don't like you meeting all these guys online. It's so sketchy."

I fought the eye roll I wanted to give her. She acted like online dating was the most absurd thing she'd ever heard of. Like millions of women get murdered by men they meet on the internet or like it was banned across the country instead of it facilitating plenty of lifelong matches.

My brother Rhett appeared behind Ashley. "Whose flowers?"

"They were just delivered for Hattie," she said, looking over her shoulder. "And I was telling her she needs to be careful with this whole online dating thing."

"Yeah. I've said the same thing." He shook his head.

Frustration coursed through me. Great. Now they were both giving me opinions I hadn't asked for.

Ashley stepped forward, dropped the bouquet onto my desk, and held the card out to me. Before I could take it, though, she snatched it back.

"Wait, is there even a signature?" Her face scrunched like she'd smelled something bad as she turned it over. "That's weird."

I let out an exasperated sigh. "They're probably from Kevin."

I'd send him a text and thank him later. But I had to admit, I was confused. Even though he was nice and our date had gone well, he'd come off as not that interested.

"Which weird dating site did you meet him on? Kill Me Over Coffee or Stab Me After Dinner?" Ashley chuckled.

Rather than amused, Rhett seemed pissed off. And I had barely told them anything. *This* was why I was considered the quiet sibling.

I narrowed my eyes. "I didn't—"

"I know you're looking for a real relationship and all," Ashley said, crossing her arms, "but I don't think this is the way to find one."

I'd actually met Kevin at a bar a few weeks ago rather than on a dating site. But I couldn't imagine these two would like that any better, so I kept that to myself. Ashley was still rambling about the dangers of online dating, so I couldn't even get a word in anyway.

"I agree." With a nod, my brother propped himself up against the doorframe.

Guess he wasn't leaving anytime soon either.

"But—"

"It's dangerous," Rhett added. "Maybe Mom can set you up with one of the single guys from church."

I slumped back in my chair. Jesus. I'd tried that last year and wouldn't again. If they'd let me get a word in, maybe I'd tell them that I was done with meeting guys online for now too. It was an easy decision after one showed up wearing a kilt, which was fine until I asked if he was Scottish, and he said no. That he just liked airing out his junk. Then another one literally never stopped smiling. Like I couldn't tell whether he had recently gotten Botox or just really liked to smile.

"I want you to find a love like I have with Jackson." Ashley tilted her head to the side as she sent me a sympathetic smile. "Creating a family with him and Sophia has made me so happy. I want that for you too. But...I don't know..." She trailed off.

I gritted my teeth. *They mean well.* I often chanted those words to myself in regard to my siblings.

Yes, I wanted to find something real. But even the guys that friends had set me up with or that I'd met while out in the last couple of years hadn't worked out. And lately the selection had gotten even more weird. At this point, I was pretty much convinced that if they were still single by the time they were thirty, then something was wrong with them.

"Maybe meet someone the old-fashioned way."

Right. Old-fashioned way. Why didn't I think of that? This time I couldn't hold back the eye roll. Not all of us had the luxury of marrying our brother's best friend like she did.

It was getting harder to deny it when my family members told me that I was picky.

If I said a guy was weird or not attentive or that I didn't feel a connection, they were quick to tell me that I wasn't giving it a fair shot.

But I could tell after one date whether there was potential. I wanted goose bumps, butterflies, and sparks. I sighed. Above all, I wanted to be seen. To be heard. With three older siblings and an over-the-top younger one, there were days when I felt somewhat invisible. Which was funny, since they never seemed to leave me alone.

"Anyway, so about tonight..." Ashley waved a hand, dismissing the conversation.

I'd said less than ten words since she showed up with the flowers. They hadn't given me a chance to respond to any of their concerns, and now we were back to talking about her.

I guess I should be thankful she was done harping on me.

"Did you hear me?" Ashley asked.

I shook my head. If she was back to ranting about my choices when it came to my dating life, I was going to throw my stapler at her. Two years ago, she made her own dumb decisions and hid her relationship and feelings for her now husband. So she really had no room to lecture me.

She huffed out a breath. "I asked if you were still coming to our New Year's Eve bash tonight."

"We'll be there," Rhett chimed in.

The two of them discussed whether Rhett and his wife, Bella, were bringing the kids. What was the point of having this conversation in my office? Obviously, they weren't really looking for my input.

I turned back to my computer and opened my email. At least I could be productive until I was summoned to speak again.

"So?"

I glanced up to find Ashley now staring at me pointedly. What had she asked? I'd already forgotten.

"Are you coming tonight?"

I ran my fingers along the silver hoop that hung from my ear. "Yeah, I'm planning to."

Though I'd rather go home after work and curl up on the couch with a book. The idea of showing up to a couples' party alone wasn't the least bit appealing. Ashley had promised there would be plenty of other single people there, but I wasn't sure I believed her. Most of my siblings and friends had either settled down and had a family or were well on their way there.

She placed her hands on her hips and rolled her eyes. "You better. Otherwise you'll work until seven and then go home and be boring."

I sighed. That was exactly what I wanted to do. But it was New Year's Eve, and even that sounded pathetic to me.

"I will be there." The promise almost hurt to make.

Finally, after the two of them rattled on about how I worked too much and I really needed to take more time off, they left my office. The conversation probably lasted less than twenty minutes, yet it left me mentally exhausted. More and more, I was understanding why my dad was so quiet. Sometimes it was easier to let everyone else say their piece. Dad only spoke up when he knew his words would penetrate through the chaos.

What I still had trouble with was not allowing their chaos to exhaust me.

I shot off a thank-you text to Kevin and got back to inputting invoices into QuickBooks.

An hour later, as I walked through the dining room of The Dock, my family's restaurant, unease wormed its way through me. Kevin had responded saying he hadn't sent flowers. I racked my brain for who else it might have been. He was the only guy I had even come close to hitting it off with recently.

"Hey, Hattie."

At the sound of the deep voice, I spun. Michael, one of the bar's regulars, was here with two other guys I recognized but couldn't name. Was one Jason, maybe?

"Hey..."

"Ashley was telling us that you have a secret admirer." Michael snickered.

My stomach sank. Of course my sister would talk about personal things like that with our customers. Small-town life was lovely. I wouldn't be surprised if a dozen more of them asked about it before the end of the week.

I shrugged. "Probably not." The last thing I wanted was to give people I barely knew any more personal information. Clearly, Ashley had told them more than enough.

Hopefully whoever sent them would send me a text, and I'd figure it out. If I didn't mention it again, Ashley would move on to something else, and the subject of the mystery flowers would be dropped.

After getting stuck chatting for a few more minutes with the regulars, I finally made my escape through the front door. I had to get better at using the side door, because every time I went this way, I got stuck talking to staff or customers. And today, I was over it all and ready to be home.

Lucky me, I still had a party to go to. I started my car, and when the low tire pressure warning light lit up on my dash, I cursed under my breath. This was ridiculous. I'd just had Randy, the town mechanic, look at the damn tire. The indicator for the front tire on the passenger side was showing low, even though he swore there was no leak. But seeing as how this would be the fourth time I'd have to put air in it, the guy had to have missed something. It was under warranty, and they'd offered to replace it. I just hadn't had time to drop it off yet.

Thankfully, it was never so low that I couldn't drive it, and usually it would go back off once I started driving.

So whatever. I wasn't dealing with it tonight. I'd call the shop sometime this week and make an appointment.

Chapter Two

DYLAN

THERE'S nothing like realizing you're the only single person left in a group of friends. I looked around Jackson and Ashley's large great room and found nothing but couples and a ton of kids.

Jesus, who invites this many kids to a New Year's Eve party? Are they all staying up until midnight?

God, I hoped not.

I wished the possibility of being surrounded by a bunch of

families had occurred to me before I'd said yes to Jackson's invitation.

He'd guilted me into coming by reminding me that since this would be my first New Year's Eve off in what felt like forever, I had to show my face at one of his parties. It wasn't like I had better things to do. Even he knew I didn't. Since I'd been promoted, working a patrol shift wasn't an option. If it had been, I could guarantee I wouldn't be here.

The only other single people I'd spied so far were Rhett's two youngest sisters, and I was *not* going there. Not only were they one of my best friend's sisters, but Savannah was nuts and Hattie was basically mute. Other than the one party here a few summers ago where she'd had a few drinks and had chatted with me, I'd hardly heard her speak.

That night, she'd been easy to talk to. Refreshing. But since then, we really hadn't interacted much. I'd started dating Becca a few months after that party, and for the last two years, she had come with me to every wedding and function I could make it to. Until now.

Now I was single and at a party among a sea of couples.

I made my way over to the bar in the corner, shaking my head. Of course Jackson would hire a bartender for a party in his own home. After ordering a beer, I shifted away from the counter so Savannah could step up.

Between the purple streaks in her blond hair, the nose ring, and the outfit made up of fishnets and strips of leather, she was *a lot*.

"Shots," Savannah yelled to the three women standing behind her.

Ah. There it was. Point proven.

Had she not gotten the memo about this being a family event? I wasn't privy to that information, so I supposed it was possible. Except she was part of this family. Did she not know all her nieces and nephews plus a bunch of other kids would be here? Even if she hadn't, she had eyes and could see.

Shots at a kids' party.

I shook my head and glanced at the other three women, hoping one of them would nix the shots. But seeing only Hattie, Jackson's sister Brittney, and another woman who looked like she was about to say *hell yeah*, I didn't have much hope.

"Oh, hello, Detective Dylan." Savannah sent me a wink.

I shifted on my feet, even more uncomfortable than I had been a second ago.

"Celeste, we need four shots." Savannah side-eyed me. "Make that five. One for the sexy detective."

I wasn't sure whether I was less surprised about Savannah being on a first-name basis with the bartender or the flirting. Either way, I'd learned over the years that Savannah did whatever she wanted and she gave no fucks about it.

Brittney sent me a quick wave, and I gave her a nod back.

"She's married," Savannah informed me as she handed me a shot glass.

I frowned at her. "Who?"

She rolled her eyes. "Brittney."

Okay. That was common knowledge around here, and even if she weren't married, there was no way I'd go there. Jackson's sister fell into the same category as Rhett's. Getting involved with a friend's sister was a terrible idea. Although apparently Jackson missed that memo. He'd married Ashley, after all.

With a nod to Savannah, I glanced over at the curvy brunette who stepped up and took a shot glass.

"Kelly's married too." Savannah sighed dramatically. "Hattie and I are the only single ladies here. Sucks to be your dick." Brow arched, she looked me up and down. "I'd totally sleep with you, though."

"Oh my god, Savannah." Hattie rolled her eyes as she sidled up next to me. "Leave the poor guy alone."

As she picked up her shot from the bar, her arm brushed against mine. On contact, my body went rigid, and I was taken back to that party a couple of years ago. To the hours we spent chatting and—admittedly—flirting.

I stole a glance at her. She was still as gorgeous as she was that summer. While her sisters were objectively good-looking, she possessed her own natural, simple beauty. If she was wearing makeup at all, it wasn't much. Her highlights were subtle, making it hard to tell whether she'd had them done in a salon or had just been out in the sun recently.

"You're making him uncomfortable," Hattie added.

I bit back a groan. At the moment, it was difficult to tell who had the honor of that discomfort—the far too brazen sister, or the sweet, irresistible one.

Savannah gave her sister a pout, but her expression quickly morphed into a wicked grin. She raised her shot glass, and the rest of us did the same. Then, once we'd clinked them all together, we threw them back.

Despite my opinion of the wild Williams sister, I couldn't deny that the burn of the tequila felt good.

Hattie held her shot glass in a strange grip, with all her fingers curled around it, almost like she was trying to hide it in her fist.

Weird. I ran my gaze over her, taking in her purple nail polish and the forced smile that was failing to hide a glimmer of annoyance.

Savannah interrupted my thoughts when she threw her hands up and moved back into the crowd.

"Come on, let's dance," she yelled over her shoulder.

Brittney and the other woman—Kelly, I supposed—followed her. Hattie, on the other hand, sighed and placed her full shot glass back on the bar.

My lips curled up. Interesting.

How did none of us notice she hadn't tossed it back when we did?

"You didn't want your drink?"

"No." She shook her head. "I'm driving home. Pretty soon, Savannah will be drunk enough not to notice when I sneak out."

I cocked my head. "Why didn't you just say no?"

"Then she would have made a stink about it." She shrugged. "I've had twenty-seven years to learn how to work my siblings."

Impressed, I grinned at her. Even I, who rarely missed anything, hadn't noticed that she didn't take the shot. Although given a few more uninterrupted minutes of perusal, I might have realized it.

"I don't want to be stuck here for longer than I have to be."

I chuckled. "Not having fun?"

"At this lovely party full of couples and kids? I'm having the time of my life," she deadpanned. "Can't you tell?" With that, she shot me a wink and walked away.

A small chuckle slipped past my lips. Damn. I'd almost forgotten that about her. She was quiet, sure, but every time I talked to her, she made me smile. Probably because it only happened once every few years. Maybe I should start remembering that.

I blinked. Wait. No. I should *not* remember that.

I was not dating the Williams sisters. Any of them—married, crazy, or mute.

Chapter Three

HATTIE

THE DOCK WAS SURPRISINGLY busy for a Tuesday in January. Usually the post-holiday fatigue that hit most of the human population in the first few weeks after the new year made restaurants seem like ghost towns. I peered into the dining room from my spot near the entrance of the back hallway where our offices were located. Today, though, it was as if most of Half Moon Lake had come in for lunch.

I couldn't fight the smile that split my face as I looked down at my nephew. It was hard to believe he was walking already. At the moment, Hudson was standing at his mom's feet and holding on to her leg, which was a good thing, with so many people in the dining room. It felt like he was born yesterday. I swear Rhett had just handed him to me to hold, and now he was toddling.

"OMG, I love blue orchids," Bella said as she bent and scooped Hudson into her arms.

Before I could ask what the heck she was talking about, one of our hostesses appeared at my side with a bouquet of white roses and blue flowers. The same type that had been delivered to me a week ago. Hopefully the person who'd sent them had signed his name this time. I never had figured out who the last set of flowers had come from. Not that I put that much effort into solving the mystery. If the person didn't care enough to tell me who they were, I wasn't wasting my time worrying about it. But now I had more, and that was weird.

"You sure seem popular lately, Hattie," Jamie said with a smile.

I winced as she bumped into Bella and the bouquet wobbled in her hand. She'd been here for longer than just about any other employee whose last name wasn't Williams, and although she could be clumsy at times, she was one of our most valued employees.

Turnover was high in our industry and always had been, but the rate at which it was happening lately had been horrible and finding decent people who actually wanted to work was even harder.

She passed me the flowers, thankfully without dropping them and turned to head back to the host stand. Bella eyed the white card, but I grabbed it out of the bouquet before she could.

It was lovely seeing you last night.

"Oh." I shook my head. "These aren't for me."

Bella not so subtly scooted closer and craned her head, so I saved her the neck cramp and handed the card to her.

"I didn't have a date last night, or see anyone, for that matter. I worked and then went home." With a pat to my back pocket, I remembered that I'd left my phone in my office. "I'll call over to Stella's and let her know they are delivering them to the wrong person."

"Here." Bella pulled her phone out of her pocket. "I have the number saved."

Of course she did. Overseeing events at The Dock made it necessary to have those contact numbers handy.

I brought up the number, and a second later, the older woman answered.

"Hi, Bella, what can I do for you?"

"It's actually Hattie Williams."

"Oh, sorry. The caller ID said Bella."

"Yeah, I'm calling from her phone."

"Well, what can I do for you?"

"I've gotten flowers delivered twice, and—"

"That's lovely, dear. I didn't realize you were seeing someone. Anyone I know?"

A heavy sigh escaped me. I didn't have much time. Rhett was going to come looking for me if I didn't hurry up. He was patient to a point, especially when it involved Bella or his kids, but if I didn't come help with the lunch rush soon, he'd be yelling my name.

"I'm not. That's the problem. I think you're delivering them to the wrong person."

She was silent for so long I pulled the phone away from my ear to make sure the call hadn't been dropped.

Finally, she hummed. "As far as I know, we haven't had any orders addressed to you."

That was exactly what I thought. "Right. They've been

delivered to The Dock. Could it be that they're meant for someone else here?"

"What kind of flowers? I can check with Archie when he gets back."

Archie. He was probably the issue. He made deliveries when one of their part-time employees wasn't available. It wouldn't surprise me if, in his old age, he was using the wrong name when he delivered them.

"I'm almost positive he didn't have a delivery for The Dock with him, though."

I bit back a chuckle. Maybe Stella was the one getting old and making the mistakes, then.

"Both bouquets were white roses and blue orchids."

Without hesitation, she said, "They didn't come from here."

My chest tightened at the certainty in her tone. "What?"

"I don't have blue orchids right now. White, red, pink, and green, but not blue."

"Maybe..." *Where else could they come from?* I racked my brain for a theory that made sense as I headed toward the hostess stand with Bella on my heels.

Rhett glared at me as I weaved through the tables, and I held up a finger to let him know I'd only be a minute.

"Jamie."

She looked over with an eyebrow raised.

I held the bouquet up between us. "Did Archie deliver these?"

A huff echoed through the line, but I ignored Stella's indignation.

With her lips pressed together, Jamie shook her head. "No. Some young kid dropped them off."

"Young kid?" My stomach sank as my mind reeled.

"Yeah." Jamie frowned, her brows pulled together. "A boy. He was maybe twelve or thirteen."

Why would a preteen boy give me flowers?

"There you go. Mystery solved," Stella chirped in my ear.

No. The mystery was not solved. At all. Was this a prank? Or...

"You have some young kid crushing on you?" Bella teased, bouncing Hudson on her hip.

"That's weird." I shook my head. "Sorry to bother you, Stella."

"Oh, it's no trouble at all, dear."

With that, I disconnected the call, handed the phone to Bella, and tossed the flowers into the trash can behind the hostess stand.

"The kid looked a little familiar," Jamie said. "I wonder if he's the Rogers boy."

I shook my head. "Nah. He's only eight." I knew that family well. Noah was the youngest and was small for his age. No way he would be mistaken for a twelve-year-old. "If you see the kid again, let me know."

"You're the boss." With a nod, Jamie turned to greet a couple who had just walked in.

Sighing, I headed toward the kitchen.

"I'll help Jamie get people seated," Bella called out. At least that was something she could do with a baby on her hip. Plus, half of our customers would fawn over Hudson. The entire town loved him.

Rhett thrust plates at me just as I stepped through the swinging door. "Run these to table ten." He turned back, grabbing the next ticket, hardly giving me time to position the plates on my arms. But years of practice gave me skills needed to balance them.

Unease hit me once again. We couldn't keep going this way. Owners and managers should be running the place, not the food. I really hoped the guy who was coming in for orientation and paperwork this afternoon was a good fit because we desperately needed the help.

After running multiple orders out and then bussing a few tables, I headed toward Bella, who was waving at me from where she stood talking with a group of young guys.

"Need help?"

She shook her head, a calculating smile turning up her lips. "No. These guys were just telling me how they're visiting from Asheville."

"Oh?" Tourists from the city were pretty common around here. What was the issue? Were they hitting on Bella? Did she need a rescue?

Before I could come up with an excuse to pull her away, she waggled her brows at me. "Yeah, and they're all *single*."

Annoyance flared hot in my veins. I expected this from my siblings, but not from my sister-in-law. But I turned to the guys and smiled.

"Half Moon Lake's pretty dull. What brings you out this way?"

I listened to their explanation about the team building exercise they were doing and how they were staying at the B&B on the water.

Finance guys from Asheville. It was hard to imagine Bella thought they were my type. But maybe I gave the vibe of loving aged-out frat boys.

For the next five minutes, I tempered my frustration and made friendly small talk, laughing about bad Wi-Fi and encouraging them to check out the local late-night bar.

"Hattie, got a minute?"

I turned, recognizing the voice instantly. Oh, thank God. Saved by the beer rep. I might not need anything special from Julie this week, but I would let her give me the rundown on every single one of her brews just for an excuse to step away.

After a twenty-minute conversation with her, I finally made

it back to my office. Smiling, listening to Rhett entertaining Hudson next door in his office, I let out a long breath and dropped into my desk chair. If I'd known that I'd be helping in the dining room for over an hour, I would have put on my flats. Heels kicked off, I leaned back, picked up my phone, and clicked on a text notification from an unknown number.

Don't throw those away.

Confusion whirled in my mind. Throw what away? I checked the time stamp. It had come through an hour ago. What had I been doing? Running food? I threw a lot of crap away. Wait...

The flowers. A chill ran down my spine, and all the breath left my lungs. What the hell?

Forgetting about my shoes, I hustled to the dining room on bare feet and scanned the patrons. No one paid me any mind. Things had slowed down considerably, but I recognized pretty much everyone here. All that was left was the regular Tuesday lunch crowd.

But an hour ago, I hadn't been paying attention.

I shifted on my feet and forced myself to take a deep breath. Maybe I was reading too much into the text.

With a sigh, I pushed the uneasiness away. I was too busy to deal with this right now, anyway. I had calls to make and an appointment with a new hire later, and then I needed to take care of his paperwork before I could leave tonight.

Finally, after crossing off every task on my to-do list, I walked back through the dining room and toward the entrance.

"Hey, didn't realize you were still here." Rhett came out from behind the bar, his keys in hand.

"Yeah. I got stuck on the phone with the liquor store, then Waylon was late for his orientation. I just finished his paperwork." I crossed my arms. "He'll be great," I added with an eye

29

roll. I was under no illusion that he'd be a valued employee. Not after he showed up late and barely paid attention to a word I said.

For months, it seemed like we couldn't find anyone who was both reliable and hardworking. Heck, we were lucky if we found a person who possessed either of those qualities.

Rhett chuckled. "Savannah said he was too busy looking at you to learn much of anything."

I shrugged. I hadn't paid the young guy much attention other than to help him fill out his paperwork. If he hadn't listed a handful of past employers, I would have sworn he'd never had a job before. Weird.

"I have two more coming in next week. Hopefully they'll work out better."

"Yeah, hopefully." It wasn't his fault. He was at least trying to find more reliable, hardworking staff.

He headed for the front doors, and I fell into step beside him.

"Hey, it's the Williams kids," Michael hollered from the other end of the bar.

In unison, we turned back and waved at the small group of regulars.

"Did you tell Tyler to cut them off?" I asked as we turned to leave.

"Yeah, and I told them they better be walking home if they don't sober up." He held the door open and gestured for me to go first. "They've been here all afternoon."

I didn't understand how people could spend hours at a bar like that. I'd be asleep on the floor.

"Then I think it's safe to say they're too drunk to drive." I shook my head as we crossed the parking lot toward our cars. "Wish we had reliable rideshare out here."

We were parked side by side, as we often were, so at my

bumper, I shuffled for the driver's door while he continued on to his own.

As I was tossing my purse onto the passenger seat, Rhett called out. "Can't drive on this tire."

Straightening, I peered at him over the hood of my car. "Huh?"

"It's flat."

Randy promised I wouldn't have any more issues out of this damn thing. Teeth gritted, I walked around the car. God, I hoped Rhett was just joking. Unfortunately, he wasn't. I slammed my fists onto my hips. "You've got to be kidding me."

"I'll take you home. I've been here too damn long to deal with changing this tonight, and if I don't get home soon, I'll miss seeing the boys before bedtime." He sighed. "I'll pick you up in the morning and deal with it then."

I huffed. "I can change a tire, you know."

"I'm not leaving you in a dark parking lot to change a tire by yourself." He ran a hand through his hair. "C'mon."

That's all it took to dissuade me. I was exhausted, and I'd argue with him over changing it myself in the morning. "Fine."

He cocked a single brow. "That was easy."

"This tire has been an issue for a while, and I don't feel like dealing with it right now either."

"Have you taken it to Randy?"

"Of course." I held back the eye roll I wanted to give him. I wasn't an idiot. "He just replaced it."

"Hmm," Rhett hummed, surveying the flat again.

Commotion from the entrance of the restaurant caught our attention, and we turned, finding one of the regulars who'd come in with Michael. I guess they were all calling it a night now that Tyler had cut them off.

"Josh, you're not driving, are you?" Rhett hollered.

Josh. That was his name. Not sure why I thought it was Jason.

"Oh." He shook his head. "No, no. I live right around the corner." With a wave, he turned and walked away.

A moment later the other guys from the bar piled out of the restaurant in a loud, rambunctious group.

With a long breath out, I turned away and climbed up into Rhett's truck.

It might not have been the most exhausting day ever, but it was pretty damn close. In fact, in these last two weeks, it had been one thing after another.

When it rains, it pours, I guess.

Chapter Four

DYLAN

As I WAITED for my name to be called, a woman sitting by the window of the small coffee shop wearing glasses caught my eye.

Hattie Williams.

My heart thumped against my sternum as her identity registered.

I wasn't sure I'd ever seen her wear glasses, but they looked cute on her. A smile crept over my lips, but I quickly locked my jaw and looked away.

Nope. She was Rhett's sister, and I could not have any kind of opinion about the sexy librarian thing she had going on.

Despite my better judgment, I peeked back for one last look. When I did, my stomach lurched. Shit. She was looking at me, probably wondering why I was gawking at her.

Now that I'd been noticed, I strode over to say hello. If I didn't, it'd only make shit weirder. "Working from the coffee shop today?" I nodded to the laptop.

"Yeah, my family is being a bit much lately." She huffed out a breath. "And Randy is working on my tire issue. Again." She tipped her head to the auto shop across the street.

I followed her gaze, slipping my hands into my pockets. "What's wrong with your tire?"

"It keeps losing air, and last night, it was completely flat."

"Just one?"

"That's the funny thing." She pressed her lips together, brows lowered behind her glasses. "It's not even the same tire. I had a new one put on last week."

My hackles rose. "That is strange."

"Yeah, that's what Randy said. He thinks the rim could be the issue rather than the tire itself." With a shrug, she peered up at me. "He said there's a slight dent, so he's going to do the soap test to verify before he replaces it."

That made sense, especially if she'd swiped a curb lately. It could be stopping the tire from sealing to the rim properly. Those issues were sometimes next to impossible to figure out.

"Order for Dylan," the barista called.

"Be right back." I hurried over to get the coffees, but halfway back to Hattie, Mrs. Jones stepped into my path.

Her feud with her neighbor was starting to grate on my nerves. She called the station at least once a month to complain about Joe next door, who was only feeding the squirrels. Our dispatcher had explained time and again that there was nothing we could do because feeding squirrels wasn't illegal. But she still called.

And now I had to listen to her rant about it, like I did every time I bumped into her, which was far too often. It took a solid five minutes for her to lose enough steam to allow me to excuse myself.

I made my way back over to Hattie. Just as I stepped up to the table, she picked up her phone, and in the next heartbeat, all the color drained from her face. Her head popped up, and she searched the small shop with wide, panicked eyes.

"What's wrong?" I asked, dropping into the seat across from her.

In a jerky motion, she turned and scoured the street outside the window. "Nothing." When she focused on me again, her chest was rising and falling rapidly. "I mean, it's probably nothing. I don't know. Just got a creepy text from an unknown number."

Every protective instinct inside me flared to life. "Really? Let me see your phone."

"Uh..." She looked at the device, worrying her lip, then back at me before finally shrugging and handing me the phone.

> I liked the purple yesterday, but that blue dress today is stunning.

"I'm not even sure it was meant for me." Her words were barely audible.

I scoffed. "Of course it's for you. They're right. You look gorgeous in that dress."

Eyes still set on me, she sucked in a breath, and for a moment, we just stared at one another, the air around us charged.

Shit. I shouldn't have said that. Not to Rhett's sister. What was it about this woman that made it impossible to not flirt with her when the two of us were alone?

I cleared my throat, needing to get us back to safer territory. "Did you wear purple yesterday?"

"Not a dress." She looked away with a huff. "But I had on a purple sweater."

I looked back down at her phone and took a screenshot, then forced my gaze back to her. "Is this the only one?"

With her brows pulled together, she shook her head. "I deleted the other one, so I can't be sure they came from the same number."

Focused on the phone again, I tapped the messages icon so I could send the screenshot I'd taken to myself. When I typed my name into the spot for a recipient, nothing came up. "Huh, kinda surprised you don't have my number."

With her head tilted to one side, she assessed me. "Why would I?"

My gut clenched. Right. Rhett's sister. Nothing more. She probably didn't make it a habit of saving the numbers of all her brother's friends in her phone.

I entered my name and number as a contact, then texted the screenshot to myself. When my phone chimed a moment later, I pulled it out of my pocket, intending to save her number in my contact list too.

Except, based on the way her name appeared along with the image, her number had already been saved. *Huh.* Had I asked for her number at that party a few years ago? The corner of my lips curled up. If I had, then it was definitely under false pretenses.

"I'll look into this for you." I blocked the random number and handed her the phone back. "But I'd bet my career this number comes back as a burner."

She shrugged. "Okay."

"Look, don't take this lightly." I narrowed my eyes and

leaned forward. "It could be nothing, but stalkers can be dangerous."

Her face screwed up into a look of disbelief. "I doubt I have a stalker. It's probably just a wrong number."

Maybe I was cynical—it was hard not to be after twelve years as a police officer—but I always erred on the side of caution when it came to this stuff.

"Regardless, be careful. And let me know if anything else comes up. I'll follow up tomorrow." With that, I stood and headed for the door.

As I strode down the sidewalk in front of the coffee shop window, she was already back to work. Though she seemed unbothered, I was left feeling like something was off. Even as I scanned Main Street, eyeing the people meandering up and down the sidewalks, I couldn't shake it.

And that uncomfortable feeling sat in my gut for the rest of the day.

Chapter Five

HATTIE

I GRITTED MY TEETH. *Come on, Savannah. Pay attention.* Instead, she was half watching TV above my head and chatting about the hockey game with the guys at the bar. I wanted to get the inventory over with, but I should have waited until Tyler was on shift.

"Jack Daniels Black Label," I said for at least the third time, leaning my side against the bar.

"Didn't we already do that one?" Savannah huffed.

"Yes, but you still haven't given me the number."

"Really?" She looked over at me, her brows pulled together.

I sighed.

"Point six," she finally said. "I don't get why we do this."

I wasn't surprised by her statement. She hated when we did inventory and made sure we all knew how useless she thought the process was.

"To keep track of waste."

"I think it's dumb."

"Yes, I'm aware." I rolled my eyes. "Ready for the next one?"

We'd only gotten through two more—Savannah had what we liked to call squirrel brain—before my sister peered over my shoulder and broke out in a salacious grin. "Hello, Detective Dylan," she purred.

Hugging the clipboard to my chest, I spun and gave him a small smile.

He returned the expression, then turned back to Savannah. "Picking up a carryout order."

"Let me go see if it's ready." She disappeared into the kitchen.

"Can I talk to you?" He rested his forearms on the bar and angled in close enough that I could smell the mint on his breath.

Things had been quiet since I'd run into him at the coffee shop a couple of days ago. Thankfully, I'd received no more flowers or texts. Even so, maybe he'd found information about the number. I'd assumed no news was good news. Now, though, he was here, so maybe that wasn't the case.

Apprehension settled in my stomach like a lead weight. "Um, sure."

"Is this the guy who's been sending you flowers?" Michael called from the other end of the bar. He and his friends had been at it again. They were clearly taking the *it's five o'clock somewhere* phrase too literally.

"Oh." I shook my head. "No."

"Flowers?" Dylan asked.

"Yeah—"

"Here you go," Savannah said as she appeared at my side. "One to-go order for the sexy detective."

Sometimes I thought my sister's life goal was to see how many people she could make feel uncomfortable. But I couldn't hide my smirk when he pretty much ignored her, keeping his gaze fixed on me as he took the bag she held out.

"Let's talk outside." The intense stare he was giving me told me not to argue.

And I wouldn't. I didn't need Savannah—any of my siblings—or The Dock's customers up in my business, so I nodded and followed him out the door.

Once the front door shut behind us, he turned to me. "Someone sent flowers to you?" His tone was sharp, his expression rigid.

"Yeah…" I crossed my arms in front of my chest.

Why did he seem so angry? I suddenly felt like a child getting ready to be scolded.

DYLAN

JESUS. I needed to chill. Instead, I was being unreasonably angry, and all because Hattie had received flowers. Women got flowers all the time. Hattie was allowed to get flowers. She wasn't mine. I had no right to be annoyed.

So why didn't it sit right with me?

"What about the phone?" Her arms were still crossed, her posture still defensive. "Isn't that why you're here?"

"Yes." Right. I came to talk to her about the phone, not to snap at her because some guy was sending her flowers. So what if she was dating someone? Good for her. I tried to relax my shoulders at that simple idea, but my body was strung tight. I needed to ignore her dating life and deal with the phone. "Definitely a burner. Bought at a gas station down the road and paid for with cash."

She shifted from one foot to the other, grimacing. "Maybe I should be worried about the flowers, then…"

Gut clenching, I searched her face, hoping to understand the meaning behind those words. "What do you mean?"

What did receiving flowers from a man she was dating have to do with the burner phone?

"I mean I wasn't even sure they were for me," she added with a shrug.

Arms crossed, I narrowed my eyes, waiting for her to explain. How did a person get flowers and not know whether they were for them? That seemed like nonsense.

She sighed and flung her arms out to the sides. "The card wasn't even signed. Or addressed to me."

My stomach twisted painfully at that admission. The flowers were from an anonymous source? *Way to bury the lede, Hattie.* It was amazing how that admission could make me both relax and stress. It didn't matter whether she wasn't dating anyone. I couldn't date her either way. So I needed to worry about the creep that was obviously stalking her.

"And no one texted me to ask about flowers they'd sent."

My eyes felt like they were bugging out of my head. "Yeah, stalkers don't typically check in with their victims."

Hattie's silky brown hair brushed her shoulders as she shook her head, not looking at all concerned about the situation. Only confusion showed in the lines of her brow. "It was all such a mystery because, according to Jamie, a young boy handed them to her and said they were for me."

"He probably slipped him some money to do it." I explained away something that didn't seem to be a mystery. A gesture like that wouldn't have seemed harmful to a kid. But who was the kid? I might be able to talk to him.

"We couldn't even figure out who the kid was. It doesn't seem like he belongs to any of the families we know."

So much for that idea.

She shrugged. "I didn't think anything of the flowers until I got a text telling me not to throw them away."

"Was that the message you said you deleted?"

She nodded. "Yeah. It came right after I threw them away." She tilted her head, her brow creasing again. "What's wrong with your face?"

"Why? Does it look like I'm having a stroke? Because that's how I feel." Rhett had always been a little oblivious, but I didn't realize it was a full-on family problem.

Her lips turned up in a smirk.

Jaw locked, I huffed. "This is not funny."

"Maybe not." She shrugged, still trying to hide a smile. "I just never realized you were so dramatic."

Was she serious right now?

"I'm not being dramatic." I balled my fists at my sides, my body taut with annoyance and concern. "You could have a stalker. There could be a person wandering out there with plans to hurt you. Yet you're laughing."

She sucked in a breath, and her eyes widened. "Are you trying to scare me?"

"Yes. Yes, I am." A little fear might help Hattie take this all a bit more seriously.

Finally, she was quiet as she stared at me. Maybe I'd gotten through to her? I shouldn't have been surprised that she was being so laid back about this. In my experience, the vast majority of people didn't understand how dangerous a stalker situation could be or how quickly it could escalate. Almost like the stalker's anonymity would keep the victim safe.

"If it was such a big deal, why did you wait two days to tell me about the phone?"

It was a fair enough question. "Remember the big fire yesterday on the outskirts of town?"

"Yeah," she said, arching one brow.

"It was declared arson. Once the blaze was out, we had to secure the scene, then wait for the state to take over."

"Oh."

"I ran the number after I saw you on Wednesday, and I would have come by yesterday if not for the fire." I cleared my throat. "But also, I didn't know about the flowers."

She cocked her head. "If you'd known about the flowers, what could you have done differently?"

"It took me twenty minutes to find out about the burner phone. If I'd had any idea you'd been receiving flowers, I could have followed up on that the same day."

"Why?"

"Because it's evidence of escalation. These things typically follow a pattern. And these patterns usually lead to the victim being hurt or kidnapped."

"But I haven't gotten another text since then."

I pinched the bridge of my nose. "'Cause I blocked the number."

"You blocked it?" She cocked her head.

Shit. I may have overstepped by doing that. Honestly, though? I hadn't really even thought about it before I did it. Just didn't want some creep continuing to bother her. Now I was reconsidering that decision. More texts could help paint a picture of what we were looking at here. It could be anything from a teenager with an innocent crush to a crazy-ass stalker that intended to do harm.

"Huh. Why didn't I think of that?"

I sighed. It was a good thing, actually, that she hadn't thought of it after the first weird text. Otherwise we would have no information to go on.

I couldn't walk away until she understood that this could be dangerous. "Hattie." I gripped her shoulder, squeezing gently. "You really need to take this seriously."

She looked up at me. Her light blue eyes held a bit of uncertainty, but at least she gave me a slight nod.

"What did Randy find when he inspected the tire?" If someone was messing with her car on top of sending anonymous flowers and weird texts, then the police needed to be involved officially.

"He put a new rim on and said I shouldn't have any more trouble. It's been fine since then."

I nodded. "If anything else weird happens—anything at all —call me, okay?"

She glanced back into the restaurant. "Everyone's staring at us now. They're going to think I'm lying about you not being the one who sent the flowers."

I scanned the group. She was right, of course. Every person at the bar was watching us. Good. Let the town gossip. I'd love it if the stalker thought she was dating a police officer. Let him come after me.

Shit. My stomach sank. I'd need to talk to Rhett, and soon. I wouldn't want him to hear from someone else that I was dating his sister.

"So you'll call me if anything else happens, right?"

"Yeah." She worried her bottom lip between her teeth. "I will."

I couldn't tell if she meant that or was just saying it to placate me. Regardless, I'd be looking into it.

Chapter Six

DYLAN

I LEFT the conversation with Hattie feeling like my head would explode and worried that though she seemed to understand my concern, she still wouldn't take the situation seriously. Yes, we lived in a small town without much crime, and maybe I was overly cautious—a byproduct of my career—but there was clearly something going on here. How had she not connected the strange texts and the flowers and maybe even the flat tire?

I slammed my carryout bag onto my desk with a huff.

Aiden, my partner, leaned back in his chair, eyeing me with apprehension. "Why are you so worked up?"

"You know the Williamses?" I turned and leaned back on my desk, crossing one foot over the other.

"Yeah."

"The younger sister?"

"The one with the purple hair?"

"No." Not sure how I forgot about Savannah. She constantly made her presence known. "The pretty one."

Aiden cocked his head. "All the Williams sisters are gorgeous."

Yeah, that was true, but neither of the other Williams women held a candle to Hattie. "Sure, but there's something about Hattie that isn't so in-your-face."

He smirked. "Uh-huh."

His tone implied that he thought there was more to my comment. But I had no intention of letting him in on my attraction to the off-limits sister. Last thing I needed was him giving me shit about it in front of Rhett. "Anyway, someone's stalking her."

"What?" He shot up straight in his seat, suddenly interested. "Stalking her?"

"Yeah." I nodded. At least someone else was taking this seriously. I would feel less stressed about it if I knew Hattie would too.

"Next time lead with that information." Aiden scoffed.

"At least I think so."

"You think?" He rested his forearms on his desk and leaned in closer.

How did I explain the conversation I'd just had with the woman who was making me feel like I was about to have a stroke at any given moment?

"My brain's on fire right now." I roughed a hand down my

face, then dove into the situation, starting with the texts and then my conversation with her about the flowers.

"And she didn't think she should be worried about it?"

"Right?" See? He was just as exasperated as I was with that tidbit of information. "Let's see if we can get the video footage from the gas station."

Aiden scoffed. "If only it were that easy."

"You never know." I shrugged. "Not like Half Moon Lake has criminal masterminds."

He chuckled. "So we're opening an official investigation?"

"Uh." Trepidation rolled through me like a wave. I didn't want to jump the gun, even though I was confident there was reason to be concerned. I needed something substantial to show Hattie before encouraging her to file a complaint. "Let's see if we can get the footage first or if we'll have to get an official subpoena and go from there."

Gut still heavy with dread, I turned back to the bag of food on my desk, though I was no longer hungry.

"What is the status of your relationship with Hattie?"

I almost dropped the container of food I had pulled out. What kind of question was that?

I spun back toward him. "Status?"

"Yeah," he said, eyes narrowed. "What is she to you?"

"Just Rhett's sister." I shook my head slightly and swallowed past the lump in my throat. Why would he imply there was something more? Wait... "Is the rumor mill talking already?"

It had been less than fifteen minutes since I'd left The Dock. I couldn't imagine news would spread so quickly.

"No. But you're looking into this unofficially, and now you're asking if I've heard rumors..."

"Nah, she's just my friend's sister." I smirked. "But I did get into an argument with her in front of half the town when I stopped by The Dock."

He cocked one brow but didn't respond.

"I don't know, man." I leaned against the desk again and dropped my head back. "She's exasperating."

"That's exactly what I thought about my wife when I met her." He chuckled. "If it turns into more, promise that you'll tell me?"

It was official. I'd completely lost my appetite. "It won't."

"But if it does?" he pushed.

"Fine." I had to appease him or I'd never hear the end of it. And it wasn't hard because I didn't cross lines like that. "But it won't."

Based on the way he was shaking his head, wearing a knowing smirk, I was surprised that he didn't call bullshit.

Chapter Seven

HATTIE

MOST DAYS, I did my best to leave work before seven, so getting out of here at six thirty on a Friday was a pretty good feat. It had been a slow, quiet night, which was strange, since the place had been packed only a few days ago.

I climbed into my car and started it up, then pulled out my phone and opened the text thread that included Savannah and Brittney, as well as Sarah and a few others who'd been added over time. Savannah and I had been close with Brittney since she'd moved to our small town in middle school. When one of the girls had added Sarah, I worried that the conversations would be awkward. Rhett had almost married her before he and Bella, who'd been dancing around each other for years, finally got together. Luckily Savannah was more interested in finding out whether Sarah's hot firefighter boyfriend had any single coworkers than she was in making the situation uncomfortable.

All the single ladies

> Me: GIF of a bottle of wine pouring into Snow White's mouth.

> Me: I totally need this after this week.

Brittney: I can come out that way tomorrow night. Margaritas at Mamacitas?

Savannah: Oh, yes. They've got a new smoking hot bartender.

I rolled my eyes. She was ridiculous.

Kelly: Totally. Let's do it. Jack is out of town this weekend.

Cece: Oh, bummer. Owen might be on shift again tomorrow, so I'll be home with the baby.

Brittney: Have they not hired another full-time guy yet?

Cece: Not yet.

Savannah: Bring her!

Cece: Grace? To a bar?

Savannah: Why not? It's not like she'll be the one drinking.

Brittney: Rachel said she can come too. She'll hold the baby.

Cece: Sarah?

Sarah: I'll ask Jay if he can stay with Nora.

I set my phone in the cupholder and pulled out of the parking lot. The moment I did, bright headlights shone through my back window as a car came out of nowhere. I didn't remember seeing anyone else leaving the restaurant, but I supposed they could have come out while I was texting the girls.

With a shrug, I turned up the radio and sang along with Taylor Swift's newest release.

As I approached a stoplight, it turned yellow. *Crap*. Wincing, I hit the gas and made a left turn. The car behind me sped up too and ran through what I had to assume was now a red light.

In a hurry much?

When I turned again and the car behind me did as well, a niggle of unease wormed its way through me. This didn't feel right. Dylan's voice echoed in my head, reminding me to take the possibility of a stalker seriously.

I was being paranoid, though, right? Letting the bossy detective and his paranoia infiltrate my mind like this?

A moment later, the car behind me revved its engine and sped up quickly, its lights blinding. With a screech, I jumped and clutched the steering wheel tight. Certain it was going to hit me, I braced myself. But the impact never came. I glanced in my rearview mirror, my whole body tense. The car, thank god, had backed off. I let out a relieved sigh.

53

AJ RANNEY

But that uneasy feeling was even stronger now, and fear had the hair on my arms standing up.

What if I did have a stalker? And now he was following me back to my apartment?

"Hey, Siri," I said. "Call..."

Shit. If I called Rhett, he'd give me a lecture on the dangers of online dating. Kyle had a very pregnant wife and two kids; I didn't want to get him involved in this. Not to mention he'd stress enough for both of us. Not exactly what I needed right now. Dylan had told me to call if any more weird things happened, right?

"Dylan," I finally said.

"Calling Dylan," the automated voice responded. A moment later, the phone rang through the car's Bluetooth.

When he picked up, I didn't give him a chance to say more than my name before I said, "This is all your fault."

He barked out a laugh. "What's my fault?"

I stole a quick glance at the car behind me. "I'm paranoid now."

"Good. You should be."

With a shaky breath, I peered into the rearview mirror again. "I think someone's following me."

"You think?" he clipped.

"I'm being ridiculous." I gripped the steering wheel tighter and straightened. "Tell me I'm being paranoid."

"I can't." There was a rustle on the other end of the line, then he asked, "Why do you think someone's following you?"

"A car pulled out of the parking lot behind me. Then it ran a red light and made the next two turns I made. At one point, it sped up so quickly I was sure it would rear-end me."

A growl rumbled through the speakers, so visceral it vibrated through me. "You're not being paranoid."

My heart plummeted. "Great."

54

"Where are you?" Clicking sounds came through the phone, like he was typing on a computer.

"I'm on Glenn Street, coming up on the elementary school."

"Turn right at Winding Way."

I made the turn, and once I'd straightened the wheel, I glanced in the mirror again. The car turned too, remaining a short distance behind me. Dammit.

Voice trembling, I asked, "Now what?"

"Irving Street. Another right."

I followed Dylan's instructions, and when the car made the turn too, I held back a sob.

"One more right at Adams."

"I'm going around in a circle." I huffed.

"Exactly. There's no logical reason for anyone to drive in a circle like that. Is the car still there?"

"Yup." Oh god. Someone really was following me. "Should I pull over?"

"No," he clipped. "Do not pull over. Do not stop."

"There's a four-way stop coming up." Not to mention several stoplights between here and my apartment.

"Roll through it," he said. "Or make another right. But do not come to a full stop."

Although I was white-knuckling the steering wheel, my hands shook. What if the person following me tried to run me off the road?

My heart, which was already pounding, took off at a break-neck speed.

"Hattie, did you hear me?"

"Yes." I nodded, even though he couldn't see me. "Do not stop." I forced a deep breath in, but when the tire pressure warning light lit up on my dash with a ding, it all escaped me along with a sharp cry. "You've got to be kidding me."

"What?" Dylan's voice was tense, harsh.

"My front tire is low. Again." What the heck? Randy promised I wouldn't have any more issues with it.

"He must be letting the air out," Dylan mumbled, like he was talking to himself.

"What?" I screeched. Blood rushed through my ears and my vision tunneled.

"Need you to stay calm, Hattie."

I scoffed. That was easy for him to say. He wasn't being followed around town by a psychopath.

"I promise I won't let anything happen to you." He chuckled softly. "Your brother would kick my ass."

I rolled my eyes, though I was thankful for the levity. "Didn't you yell at me earlier for laughing?"

"Yes. But now I'd rather make you laugh than let you spiral into a panic."

"I'm not panicking." I left off the *yet* part of that statement.

"You're not far from Kyle's house," he said. "Head there."

"No. I'm not leading the stalker to Kyle and Tina's. They have two kids and another one on the way."

The last thing I wanted to do was get my family involved in this. I'd never hear the end of it. Maybe this was what I deserved for trying to meet people on the internet. I'd picked up a stalker.

"Fine. Come here, then."

I blinked at the infotainment screen, where Dylan's name was lit up. "What?"

"I live a couple of blocks from Kyle's, so I'm the next closest option you have."

"Maybe I should just go to the police." The station was less than ten minutes from here.

"I agree." He sighed. "That's why I said come here."

"Here? I thought you said the police—"

"I am the police," he interjected. "Come to me."

"Oh, I meant the police station." Though his house *was* closer, and I wouldn't have to worry about any stoplights.

"Hattie..."

His voice had that bite again, the one that made it clear he expected me to obey. Was that his cop voice? Despite being irritated by his demand, I couldn't stop the shiver that coursed down my spine.

"Kyle's house or mine. Pick one. Those are the only choices you've got."

How had I not noticed this side of him in the twelve years I'd known him? In any other situation, I would have pushed back against his bossiness. Right now, though, I was desperate to get to safety. I looked into the rearview at the car still following me and gripped the steering wheel even tighter.

"Fine. How do I get there?"

DYLAN

I breathed a sigh of relief as her headlights shone down my street.

"You see me?" Standing on my front lawn, I waved a hand.

"Yeah." Her voice trembled, but she wasn't panicking.

I hated how scared she sounded, but I was impressed by her levelheadedness.

"You're almost here. Doing great," I said. "Pull into my driveway."

She'd barely come to a stop, the back of her car still in the road, before she threw the door open and darted straight toward me.

I opened my arms and brought her tight against my body.

She shook with adrenaline and fear, her breaths coming in gasps now. Fuck. I'd never wanted to punch a wall—or better yet, the asshole following her—more than I did in that moment.

This prick was messing with the wrong person.

I tightened my hold around her as the dark-colored vehicle sped up and flew past my house.

"7KL4TBC."

"What?" she whispered against my chest.

"License plate." I repeated the digits in my head as I pulled my phone out and texted Aiden, asking him to pull the registration for a Toyota with this license plate.

"I need to call this in."

She pulled back and peered up at me, her eyes glassy. "What?"

"He's escalating. I need to get the department involved so we can start an investigation."

I didn't plan to mention the possible dead end we'd hit with the gas station. According to the attendant, the surveillance cameras only held on to a recording for so long before it was erased to make space for new footage. The guy didn't know how to access it or how long footage was saved, so we planned to go back tomorrow to speak to the owner.

She nodded and blew out a shaky breath. "Okay."

"That means you need to tell your family." I pulled back and gripped her shoulders, forcing her to look at me.

"Now?"

"It's no skin off my back if they hear about your stalker from someone else—and you know they will; you know how this town is—but is that what you want?"

She shifted her weight and sighed. "No. Especially my parents."

I nodded. "Come on, I'll drive you over."

Lips pressed together, she nodded. "I guess it'll look like I'm being responsible if I show up with the police."

I couldn't help but smirk at her reasoning.

It faded quickly, though, as uneasiness settled in my gut. Wrapping an arm around her shoulders, I led her toward my SUV.

Chapter Eight

DYLAN

THIS WAS DEFINITELY NOT how I thought this would go. I didn't anticipate having to answer to anyone but Hattie's parents, since she wanted to hold off until tomorrow to tell her siblings. But as luck would have it, Rhett happened to be here too, glaring at me.

Hattie, of course, was already trying to downplay the situation.

This woman would be the death of me.

"Really. It's probably nothing, but Dylan wants to be safe

and look into it." Hattie shrugged. "I doubt he'll find anything. It's hard to believe anyone would actually stalk me."

All I could hope was that Hattie was minimizing the issue for her parents' sake.

"Can we talk?" Rhett stepped up next to me, nodding toward the kitchen. My stomach sank at the idea that he was going to grill me about exactly why I was here with Hattie. With as easily as Aiden had seen through my denial of my attraction to her, I worried Rhett might too.

But without waiting for a response, he headed out of the room.

Once I stepped through the doorway, he spun on his heel, glowering. "Need you to do me a favor."

"I'm already looking into it." Obviously.

He raked a hand through his dark hair. "I know...but I want you to stay with her. Make sure she's safe."

"What?" My lungs seized up. The idea of staying with her was both a thrill and torture. I wasn't sure I could trust myself to be around her that much. I could still feel her body against mine as she'd hugged me. At the moment, I was half-focused on the stalker, but now... Nope couldn't go there. "You realize I have a job, right?"

Currently, we had no active cases—that would change once we got the official paperwork going on this one—but that didn't mean I didn't have other duties to see to or that another one couldn't pop up at any time.

"I can't be with her all the time," I clarified. For many reasons, not just work.

He nodded. "She's fine when she's at work. I'll be there. I'll have Tyler keep an eye out too. But I don't want her alone in her apartment, and she's too stubborn and independent to stay with any of us."

He made a good point, I supposed. I didn't like the idea of her being alone in her apartment halfway across town either.

Even so, if I agreed to this, then I couldn't take lead on her case. The person who took point would need to run down any lead, no matter when it popped up.

"Besides, she'll feel comfortable with you. She's known you since she was, what, fifteen?"

I met Rhett shortly after I'd graduated from the police academy and moved to Half Moon Lake. The crowd he'd run with back then had welcomed me in pretty quickly, and I'd spent plenty of time around his family too. So yeah, he was probably right on that front. Though it was hard to believe that the same awkward, timid teenager I'd met when I moved here was the woman currently making my head spin.

"She probably sees you as another overprotective brother," he added.

I flinched. God, I fucking hoped that wasn't how she saw me. I sure as shit didn't see her like a sister. My heart lurched at the thought. Shit. It really didn't matter because, either way, I wasn't going there.

"Please, man." Rhett frowned, his face etched with concern. "She's my little sister."

A long sigh escaped me. "Let me see what I can do." I'd have to talk to Aiden before I could make any promises. "I've gotta make a phone call first. In the meantime, do me a favor."

"Anything."

I smirked. "If you hear any rumors about me dating Hattie, go along with it."

His eyes popped wide. "What?"

And that glare was back.

"Half the town saw us talking outside The Dock earlier. We were discussing the troubles she's been having, but it seems as though the interaction was misinterpreted. And honestly, it could work in our favor if the stalker finds out that Hattie is dating a police officer."

It could also push the guy to escalate more quickly, but I'd keep that to myself. While it was a distinct possibility, the quicker that happened, the more likely he would be to mess up.

For a long moment, Rhett studied me. Finally, he huffed. "You better not be trying to tell me you're dating my sister."

I scoffed. "I'm not—"

"Good. 'Cause the last thing she needs is relationship drama."

I raised one eyebrow. "Drama?"

"Yeah, man. It follows you wherever you go. All your relationships turn dramatic, and they never end easily."

I locked my jaw. He wasn't wrong about the drama, though I wasn't the cause. The last two serious relationships I'd been in, and even the more casual ones, had come down to one issue. My career choice. I had yet to find a woman who could handle my job. The hours. The danger.

"What I'm saying is that it's a good thing if the stalker thinks we're dating."

He nodded. "Okay. I've got some papers for my dad to sign, then I need to get home to Bella and the kids." He stepped around me and put a hand on my shoulder. "Thanks for looking out for Hattie, man."

"Of course."

Once I was alone in the kitchen, I dialed Aiden.

"Hey," he started. "The plates came back stolen."

Irritation flared in my gut, though I wasn't surprised. "I figured as much."

"Weren't you the one who said we don't have criminal masterminds here?"

I chuckled. "Anyone who watches TV knows not to use a car registered to them to commit a crime."

"Truth."

"Gonna need you to take lead on this."

"What?" He scoffed. "I assumed you'd want the lead."

"Rhett asked me to stick close to Hattie, so I can't be available as often as I'd need to be if I were."

"You're sure there's nothing going on between you two?"

"Yeah, I'm sure."

He let out a loud sigh, the sound muffled through the line. "Okay. I'll talk to the captain before I leave and see if we can pull Ethan to help out with this one."

That was a great idea. Ethan was a great patrolman. Eventually, he'd make detective if he wanted it. If I was watching Hattie, we would need help anyway. Aiden had a wife and kid. Asking him to do all the legwork would be a dick move. Plus, if I needed to take over for any reason, Ethan could keep an eye on Hattie.

"Okay, and I'll bring Hattie by the station tomorrow to give her official statement. Talk to you again in the morning."

A minute later, after I'd hung up with Aiden, Hattie entered the kitchen through the open doorway.

"Dylan?"

"You ready to go?"

She nodded, exhaustion marring her features. "Yeah. It's late."

The frightened woman from earlier was gone. Either she was holding her shit together and putting on a brave front, or she was back to being in denial.

Regardless, we needed to have a conversation. These next few days were crucial. The stalker was likely angry that his plans tonight had been thwarted. With any luck, he would decide I was the problem and come after me next.

Chapter Nine

HATTIE

I FIDDLED with the silver beaded bracelet my mom had given me for Christmas last year—the one that matched the bracelets she'd given my sisters as well. It gutted me, seeing the worry on her face tonight. Though that sensation was replaced by annoyance when, as I was assuring my parents that it was probably nothing, Dylan sent me a glare.

I couldn't fathom who would want to stalk me.

None of the guys I'd dated recently had been any more interested in me than I was in them. Except maybe the guy who asked if I would let him suck my toes. But even he quickly became uninterested when I told him he absolutely could not. Not to mention, stalkers were for famous people or people like Savannah, who were attention seekers, not run-of-the-mill people like me.

"I'm going to pack a small bag," Dylan said as he pulled out of my parents' driveway. "Then I'll follow you to your apartment."

"What?" I whipped my head around and frowned. I wasn't all that excited to get back in my car, but I didn't need a babysitter.

"You shouldn't be alone." He shrugged, one hand on the steering wheel while the other one rested between us on the console. "Rhett asked me to stay with you until we catch this guy."

Of course my idiot brother would ask him to do that. And without running it past me first. "That's not—"

"Unless you'd rather stay with one of your siblings or at your parents' until this is over?" He looked over with one eyebrow raised.

"My older siblings all have kids, so no, I'm not leading a stalker to their front door. And Savannah is never home, so staying with her would be no different from staying alone."

As far as my parents went? My mom would worry enough for the two of us, and I didn't handle that kind of thing well. Ashley was the mom whisperer, not me. I never truly knew what to say or do.

"That's what I thought."

"So, what? You're going to sleep on my couch every night?"

"Yeah. Unless..." He side-eyed me. "You could stay at my place. I have a guest room and security cameras."

With a huff, I shook my head. Of course he had security cameras. Never in my life had I thought about needing something like that. We lived in a small town, for Christ's sake. We rarely saw more than a little shoplifting from the corner store or the occasional drunk driver or domestic abuse situation.

With my head pressed against the seat, I tipped my face up and closed my eyes. All I wanted was to go to bed. If he wanted to spend the night on my couch, then more power to him. We could work through the logistics tomorrow. Maybe in the light of day, I could convince him that I was fine on my own. I swallowed thickly. Is that what I wanted, though? The thought of being alone in my apartment sent fear tingling down my spine again.

"Could we leave my car at your place and come back for it tomorrow?"

Saturdays were pretty uneventful for me, so it shouldn't be a big deal.

He turned and gave me a quick once-over before focusing on the road again. The look was enough to send heat creeping up my neck. But my mind and body were heavy with exhaustion, and I really didn't feel up to getting back in my car right now.

"Sure."

Ten minutes later, I took in the details of his living room, surprised by how tidy it was. There wasn't a single article of clothing hung over the back of a chair, and there was no clutter. Not even a stack of mail on the entryway table. Now that I was witnessing the way he lived, I was nervous about bringing him back to my place. It was clean, but I was not good at keeping the clutter to a minimum. Clothes always hung over furniture, mail collected on my counter, and shoes tended to pile up by the front door.

I was still examining the room when Dylan appeared with a backpack slung over his shoulder. "Ready to go?"

I nodded, and then we were heading to my apartment.

"Tomorrow," he said, glancing at me from the driver's seat,

"we need to sit down and talk. I'm going to need names of anyone you've met or talked to in the last six months."

"Okay." I cocked my head, beginning a mental list. It would be a chore to recall some of the names. I'd been on a mission to find Mr. Right, but hadn't been successful. More than anything, I'd met a string of men who were altogether forgettable. "Might be easier if I give you my login information."

Brows pulled low, he studied me. "For what?"

"For the dating apps I've been using."

He scoffed and shook his head. "Are we talking *Tinder*?"

"Ew, no." What kind of girl did he think I was? "More like *eHarmony*, *Match* and *Bumble*." I rolled my eyes. "Let me guess, you're going to lecture me on the dangers of online dating now?"

"Nah. The security and tracking capabilities of those apps are a whole lot better than they used to be." At the stop sign down the street, he looked over at me. "But I'll need you to think about people here in town. Anyone who has shown interest in you, even if you haven't reciprocated."

That was easy. The list was nonexistent. I couldn't think of a single guy who'd paid me *that* kind of attention. At least not recently. But I nodded anyway.

As we entered my apartment, I collected the shoes and a few items of clothing scattered around the living room.

"Sorry it's messy. I haven't had time to straighten up this week."

I eyed my small sofa, a pit forming in my stomach. I was a jerk, I realized, for expecting Dylan to squeeze his six-foot frame onto the thing. Then again, I hadn't asked for a babysitter.

"No worries." He tossed his backpack onto the armchair closest to him as I headed down the hall toward my bedroom.

Once I'd stashed all the items I'd picked up in my bedroom,

I returned, finding Dylan on the sofa with his laptop balanced on his legs.

"Do you mind writing down those sites and your login information for me? I'm going to start making a list."

"Sure." I grabbed a pen and piece of paper from the drawer in the kitchen and pulled out my phone to look up the usernames and passwords I had saved. "Here you go." After handing him the information, I shifted my weight and yawned, feeling like I'd just run a marathon. "Need anything else before I head to bed?"

"I'm good." He studied me silently for a moment, then dipped his chin. "Get some rest."

Ten minutes later, I fell into bed, and I was out in a matter of seconds. When I woke again, it was dark, and I was thirsty. I usually kept a glass of water on the nightstand, but I'd been too tired to remember to bring one to bed with me. I padded barefoot toward the kitchen. As I passed the bathroom door, it opened, and I jumped a foot in the air.

"Shh, it's just me." Dylan stepped out without a shirt, instantly distracting me from the fear that had flared inside me a second ago. There was no room for it now. Not with the way I couldn't stop myself from taking in his broad shoulders and chest and his toned abs.

My stomach flipped. Damn, was the man fit.

It was so much easier to ignore how hot he was when he had a girlfriend or when we were in a group. Now, standing a foot in front of me, alone in my apartment and shirtless, he was impossible to pull my eyes away from.

I drank him in slowly, moving my gaze up. When I made it to his face and found him inspecting me as well, my skin heated. His pupils dilated as he zeroed in on my chest.

Shit, I wasn't wearing a bra, and I was dressed in nothing but a thin tank top and sleep shorts. I crossed my arms over my chest, and he cleared his throat, breaking his heated perusal.

I was definitely not used to having guys stay over, especially ones I wasn't hooking up with. Who was I kidding? I couldn't remember the last time *any* guy spent the night.

"Sorry," I muttered. "Just came out to get a glass of water."

I brushed past him and into the kitchen. I'd definitely need to add ice to the water to cool myself down.

Maybe his place would have been a better choice. At least there, we would have had our own rooms and probably separate bathrooms too.

With a harsh breath out, I resigned myself to accepting that offer tomorrow. How long could it take to catch a stalker anyway? I could stay with him for a few days. His house was closer to work and the police station than my apartment was, so why not?

Water glass in hand, I shuffled back to my room, murmuring a quick good night to Dylan, who was settling in on the couch. Once I was back in bed, I sighed and forced my mind to calm.

We could figure it out tomorrow.

Chapter Ten

DYLAN

THIS WAS GOING to take longer than I expected. Between the three apps Hattie was using, the list of guys she'd had contact with was extensive. Although it looked like she'd only gone out with about twenty of them in the last six months, the number of messages was absurd.

Then again, the woman was gorgeous, so I couldn't blame any of these men for reaching out. Why wouldn't she have a shit ton of men vying for her attention? An image of her in the tiniest tank top and shorts I'd ever seen popped into my head unbidden, pulling a groan from me. Fuck, the way her nipples had pebbled against the fabric—

"Good morning," Hattie said, startling me from my dirty thoughts. Her voice was husky from sleep, but at least she had more clothes on than the last time I'd seen her. Though the oversized sweatshirt barely covered the tiny-ass booty shorts she sported.

"Good morning. How'd you sleep?"

With a shrug, she propped one shoulder on the doorframe between the kitchen and living room. "Okay, I guess. You?"

Like shit. But I kept that to myself. Squeezing my six-foot frame onto her small couch hadn't been the least bit comfortable. Then, after running into her in the hallway, I couldn't get the image of her out of my mind.

"Fine," I replied instead. "We need to go over this list of names I put together." I held up my notepad.

"Coffee first." Yawning, she shuffled into the kitchen. "You want a cup?"

I nodded. "Sure. Thanks."

After she brewed two cups and poured a splash of cream into hers, she held up the bottle. "Want cream? Or sugar?"

"Black is fine."

Her nose scrunched up in the cutest way. "Gross. But okay." With both mugs in hand, she carefully headed into the living room and handed one to me.

I set the piping hot liquid on her coffee table to give it a moment to cool and picked my notepad back up.

She took the spot next to me and placed her coffee beside mine while she looked over the list. "Um..." With her head tilted to the side, she sat shoulder-to-shoulder with me and studied the list. "Can we look at their profiles?"

"What?" Massaging my forehead, I sighed.

She shrugged. "I'm not sure I remember half these guys."

"You don't remember the guys you went on dates with in

the last six months?" Looking over the list, there were a lot of names. But to not remember, the dates must have been awful. I shouldn't like the idea that she'd been disinterested in all of them, but I felt a hair lighter anyway.

"I can't remember all their names. Honestly, I'm not even sure I knew some of their last names. I'd recognize their pictures, though. But the truth is, most of these guys were that forgettable."

The last thing I wanted to do was go through the damn apps again. But determined to get through this as painlessly as possible, I navigated to my web browser and pulled up the first dating site.

Almost an hour later, we had gone through the names and I'd added half a dozen more to the list. Guys she'd either talked to on the phone from the app but hadn't gone out with or that she'd met off-line. This was a good starting point, though I had enough experience to know it likely wouldn't be simple to narrow this list down.

Her phone buzzed in rapid succession from the kitchen counter, so with a sigh, she stood and darted for it.

"Dammit." She groaned as she turned toward me. "I forgot I'm supposed to meet the girls for margaritas at Mamacitas tonight."

"They'll understand why you can't come." I didn't look up as I said it, but I was met with nothing but silence. The heat of her gaze burned into me, finally forcing me to look at her. Sure enough, she was sending me a death glare. I leaned back on the sofa and crossed my arms over my chest, waiting for her argument.

"I never said I wasn't going."

For a beat, I was speechless. She couldn't possibly be serious. My lips tightened into a firm line as she blinked at me, waiting.

"There's a psychopath out there that might be trying to

hurt you…or worse." I tossed my hands in the air. Keeping her safe was going to be a hell of a thing if she didn't even try to work with me. "I figured that staying away from bars was implied."

She fisted her hands on her hips, her eyes narrowing further. "I'm not going to stay locked up in my apartment for the next week."

I scoffed. Now she was just being dramatic. "I didn't say that. But a night out at a crowded bar is not worth the risk."

"That's your opinion, but in this situation, that's for me to decide. Isn't it?"

Jaw locked, I breathed in and out through my nose. "I'm in charge of your safety, so I get to decide."

She crossed her arms over her chest. "Yeah, and how do you plan to stop me?"

Standing, I matched her glare. "I could start by handcuffing you to your bed."

Her breath hitched, and her eyes widened, pupils dilating. *Fuck.* Would she like that kind of thing? My heart hammered in my chest. I could see it. Her in those tiny-ass shorts waiting for me. But in my mind, it was my bed she was locked to. And I'd make sure she fucking loved it.

I blinked. What the hell? Where had that come from? Obviously it shouldn't matter whether she'd like it. She was Rhett's sister. I cleared my throat and banished the thought. "How about we compromise?"

A night out with her friends would be a great way to decrease her stress and give her a chance to forget about the danger she was in for a little while. I understood that. But a crowded bar? No way.

She huffed. "I'm listening."

"Why don't you invite them here instead?"

She immediately opened her mouth, but before she could argue, I raised a hand.

"I'll sit outside in my car and keep an eye out."

There was only one way into her apartment building, whereas Mamacitas had multiple points of entry.

She stared at me for a long minute before finally letting her shoulders relax. "Fine."

At the sound of a dog barking nearby, I strode to the window and peered through the blinds. A man with a black lab on a leash stood nearby. The dog was barking incessantly in the direction of the trees that lined the edge of the parking lot.

My gut instinct didn't like it. But a second later, the dog stopped and turned its attention away.

"Everything okay?"

I turned back to Hattie and nodded. "Yeah. Just a dog." I was on high alert, but that could have been nothing, so there was no reason to worry her unnecessarily. "Did you want to head to my place to get your car?"

She sighed. "Yeah, if the girls are coming here, then I'll need to get snacks and stop by the liquor store."

I adjusted my holster on my hip, the movement catching her attention. She homed in on my hand, her eyes widening as if she'd only now realized I was wearing it under my T-shirt.

With a wave of my hand, I looked her up and down. "You might need actual clothes for that."

She rolled her eyes. "Yeah, I didn't plan on going out in my pajamas."

Pajamas? Those shorts were more like underwear than pajamas.

"Go get dressed." I nodded toward her room. "We can grab breakfast before we get your car."

With her hands on her hips again, she huffed. "Anyone ever tell you you're bossy?"

"Yep, all the time." I shrugged. I wouldn't apologize for it either. Any decent cop was. It was imperative that we know how to manage and control a situation.

"You're ridiculous." With the most adorable growl, she spun on her heel and stomped down the hall. "I'll just be a few minutes."

I tore my gaze away from her long, lean legs, thankful as fuck it was too cold for her to leave the apartment in a pair of shorts.

Chapter Eleven

HATTIE

I COULDN'T STOP THINKING about Dylan handcuffing me to my bed. Jesus. What was wrong with me? I had a stalker, and instead of being worried about being attacked—or worse—by the unknown person, I was getting all hot and bothered by the dirty thoughts about the cop trying to protect me that kept creeping into my head.

It was like the plot of a bad lifetime movie. Spoiler alert: The stalker will end up being from one of the dating apps.

Poor Hattie Williams will be a lesson to all the single women in Half Moon Lake. And I'd never hear the end of it from my siblings.

Dressed and ready for the day, I stepped back into the living room. Dylan looked ready in a pair of jeans that hugged his thick thighs and tight ass. His T-shirt stretched taut across his shoulders as he slipped his laptop back into his bag. The outline of his gun under his shirt caught my eye as he shifted. Had he been wearing it last night? If so, how hadn't I noticed when I clung to him in his yard? Regardless, his presence here made me feel safe.

"You ready?" He looked up at me.

With a nod, I tucked my phone into the back pocket of my jeans. "Yeah." I snagged my keys and the small wallet attached from the counter, then followed Dylan toward the door.

"Fuck." He pulled up sharply, grasping the doorknob, his focus trained on the floor in the hall.

I peered around him, and my heart dropped. "What..."

Outside my door was a bouquet of wilted blue orchids.

No. No, no, no. This wasn't happening.

He slammed the door, turned the dead bolt, and spun, his jaw rigid and his eyes hard. "Go pack a bag."

"What?" I gaped at him, struggling to form coherent thoughts. God, I wished what I'd seen was a hallucination. Instead, it was evidence that the stalker knew where I lived.

Dylan stepped up close, the movement pulling me from my stupor. "I need to call this in, but we're not staying here." He gripped my shoulder. "He's escalating, and my place has cameras."

I opened my mouth, but closed it without saying a word. No way was I going to argue with him. Glancing up and meeting Dylan's intense stare, I nodded.

"Hattie," he said softly. "It's gonna be fine."

I wasn't sure about that. None of this felt fine.

Without thinking, I stepped forward and burrowed into him. When he wrapped his arm around me and held me tight, I melted against his body. There, for a moment, I could believe his words. That everything would be fine.

He loosened his hold, and I stepped back, peering up at him. Why was this happening? Why me? It had always been easy for me to hide in a crowd. I could quietly leave a room, and no one would bat an eye. I'd never been like my sisters, who drew attention with their loud, outgoing personalities.

Now, though, someone was hyper focused on my every move.

"I'll go get my stuff." Sighing, I turned and headed to my room.

After grabbing what I needed for a week at Dylan's, I came back out to find Aiden standing in my living room.

"Still no hits on the car?" Dylan asked.

Aiden shook his head. "No, but I have officers searching the woods in case he's on foot."

Dylan crossed his arms in front of his chest. "He's taking a lot of risks."

"Yeah, especially if he knew you were in here. That's some ballsy shit."

"That's what worries me."

Dread settled in the pit of my stomach. Suddenly, I worried that the stalker would not be deterred by Dylan. Would I even be safe at his place?

Aiden glanced over Dylan's shoulder and nodded in my direction. "Hey, Hattie."

Dylan spun, his gaze softening as he spotted me. "You have everything you need?"

"I think so."

He closed the space between us and took the large duffel from me. Then he turned back to Aiden. "Keep me posted."

"Will do."

I followed Dylan out to his car. The police officers canvasing the area made my heart beat faster. But I didn't want to look ridiculous about it, so I fisted my shaking hands and tried to be calm. Once I was in the front seat and we were headed away from my apartment building, my heart finally slowed down. Knowing Dylan was right next to me, I began to relax. Even if the stalker tried to get close to me again, I had to believe he would protect me.

My phone vibrated, and when I pulled it out and checked the screen, I groaned. Dammit. I'd definitely have to cancel with the girls tonight. The whole thing made me angry. First, we couldn't go to the bar, and now I couldn't even have them at my place.

"What is it?" Dylan raised a brow but kept his focus on the road.

As I tapped out a reply, I said, "It's the girls. Need to tell them I can't meet up tonight."

"Don't." He put his hand on my phone, pausing my movements. "Invite them to my place. There's plenty of room for you to chill."

I gaped at him. Why on earth would he want me to do that? Heck, why was he doing any of this? Loyalty to my brother, I understood, but only to a degree.

"Do you know what you're agreeing to?" I chuckled. "Savannah is a bit much."

"A bit?" His lips tipped a fraction.

Fair enough. But again, why would he want my over-the-top, loud-ass sister hanging around his house? Just invading his space for the next several days was bad enough. I considered him, studying his strong jawline, his sharp nose, trying to figure him out.

"It's fine. I can handle her." He shrugged. "It'll take your mind off all this bullshit."

My heart stuttered at the sincerity in his words, at the thoughtfulness of the offer. It had been a very long time since anyone had truly paid attention to what I wanted or needed. Of course I wasn't always the best at vocalizing it either.

Swallowing thickly, I ducked my head and typed out a new message.

All the single ladies

Me: I have good news and bad news.

Savannah: Bad news first so we can chase it with the good.

Me: Bad news is my apartment is a crime scene now, so hanging out there is out of the question.

Me: But the good news is that Dylan offered his place instead.

Savannah: Oh did he? That's interesting.

Brittney: Wait, back up. Why is your apartment a crime scene?

Savannah: Who cares? We get to hang out at the sexy detective's house.

Brittney: I do. I'm worried about why my friend's apartment is a crime scene. Do you need bail money, Hattie? Are you okay? Do we need to kick someone's ass?

Rachel: 😂 I love how you assume she broke the law.

Savannah: I'm at work with Rhett, so I can confirm that she didn't kill him for asking his best friend to stay with her. Though she could have killed Dylan, I guess. But that would be a shame. He's too fucking mouthwatering.

Me: I did not kill anyone. Stalker showed up and left wilted flowers outside my door.

Rachel: Fuck, that isn't good.

Cece: Wait, wasn't Dylan there with you?

Savannah: That raises a good question...
Were you two distracted?

Me: 😳 yes, actually. We went through my dating history over the last six months. He probably thinks I'm desperate.

Savannah: Or that you're not willing to settle for a tool bag.

Brittney: Yay for not killing someone. Sorry about the stalker situation, and I agree with Savannah about not settling. Set that bar high. Why not shoot for that sexy detective? 😏

Me: You guys are ridiculous. Nothing is going to happen between Dylan and me.

Cece: Famous last words.

I SET my phone down and stole a glance over at Dylan. I couldn't deny he was extremely good-looking. Tall, with dark features, a chiseled jaw, and muscles—lots of muscles—without an ounce of fat. I hadn't really noticed him in that way until more recently. I was only fifteen when he first moved here, but by the time I was in my early twenties, it was hard not to notice how attractive he was.

As if he sensed my perusal, he looked over. Quickly, I pulled my gaze away and spun the bracelet on my wrist.

Nothing was going to happen with my brother's best friend. Regardless of how sexy he was.

Chapter Twelve

DYLAN

I DIDN'T KNOW what to expect, but being surrounded by the deafening laughter of seven women as Savannah acted out a date she'd recently been on was not it.

"Totally lame. He danced like this." Savannah moved her body in jerky motions that made it look like she was doing a mix of the twist and the floss.

I shook my head. She was, without a doubt, nuts.

From the kitchen table where I sat with my laptop, I had a good view of them in the sunroom at the back of the house. I wasn't eavesdropping. There was no need with how loud they were.

Hattie had been hesitant of being so out in the open but had relaxed and warmed to the idea when I explained that I had cameras that would alert me to movement anywhere around my house. I wasn't worried as long as the women listened if I told them to move.

"Are we betting on how long it'll take for Hattie and Detective Delicious to hook up?"

I leaned forward, intent on hearing the responses, especially Hattie's. That was not happening, but it didn't stop my curiosity.

"Savannah," Hattie bit out. "Cut it out. He might be able to hear you."

She straightened in her seat and turned, so I quickly looked down at my computer.

"Interesting. She didn't deny that it's a possibility. My bet is a week." That comment was from the redhead Hattie had introduced as Rachel.

"You guys are way off base." Hattie scoffed. "And give me more credit. I have way more self-restraint than that. Jeez."

"Have you seen the ass on the detective?" Rachel chuckled.

I shifted, uncomfortable with where this line of conversation was going.

"A week is more than I would have given you."

"Seriously, Savannah." Hattie's voice was a harsh whisper now, so I couldn't hear what followed.

Dammit. As she spoke, I studied her. Her posture was less tense than it had been earlier, but there was a flush creeping up her face now.

My phone vibrated on the table, so, chuckling at Hattie's clear embarrassment, I picked it up. The notification on the screen showed a text from my neighbor.

Logan: You having a party over there?

Me: I wish. All work, no play.

Logan: Maybe I'm in the wrong job, then. My gig as a firefighter has never led to having a bunch of beautiful women hanging out at my house.

Me: Half of them are married. I'm helping a friend out by watching his sister. She has a stalker.

Logan: Oh shit, you for real?

Me: You have the kids this weekend?

Logan: Nope and not on shift. Want to invite me over for a beer and introduce me to the single ones?

TEETH GRITTED, I glared at my phone. Hell no. I had no claim on Hattie, nor should I want to claim her, but introducing her to Logan? The idea irked me. Though...as another thought popped into my head, I couldn't help but smirk.

Me: Sure, come on over. Savannah, the blonde dancing on the chair right now, seems like fun.

Logan: She might be too wild for me. I'm an old man now.

I scoffed. He was thirty-two, the same age as I was. We were *not* old. Though maybe a marriage and subsequent divorce and co-parenting two kids made Logan feel older some days.

> Me: Maybe young and free is what you need.

> Logan: Be right over.

Aiden's name flashed on the screen before I could set my phone down, so I quickly accepted the call. "What's up?"

"Talked to the manager at the gas station."

Frustration bubbled up, and my jaw ticked. The plan had been for him to do that this morning, but then it was thrown to the back burner when the orchids were left at Hattie's door. I wasn't available to help at all today either, adding more to my frustration.

"Tell me you have something."

He sighed. "Wish I could."

I pinched my eyes closed. Not the news I wanted.

"Their surveillance system only saves a month of footage..."

"And since the phone was purchased in November, we're screwed." I finished for him.

"Pretty much."

I pressed a palm to my forehead. For a moment, I just breathed and thought through what we knew so far. Straightening, I cleared my throat. "Ask him to call when another one is purchased."

"What?"

"I blocked the number on Hattie's phone. If he's watching

her and notices that when he sends a text, she doesn't check her phone, he'll catch on and want to purchase a new one."

"That's a long shot."

My stomach knotted painfully. "Maybe," I said, "but it's what we have right now. He risked setting those flowers outside her door, so why not this? Maybe we'll get lucky."

"I'll reach back out to the manager tomorrow. It wouldn't hurt for them to keep us in the loop."

"Thanks, man. I narrowed down the list of names Hattie and I created this morning." After she went through the original list, I moved the ones who lived close to the top and removed those who no longer lived in the state. "Getting ready to send it over."

From here, we'd split the names and do a deep dive into each one to see if we could connect one of them to the gas station where the burner was bought or the Toyota Corolla that had followed her last night.

"Okay. I'll check back in tomorrow."

Just as I ended the call, my phone buzzed with a notification from my camera app. Someone was approaching the front door. I double-checked to confirm it was Logan, then stood and strode for the front door.

HATTIE

"I HATE YOU RIGHT NOW." Savannah sighed and sat back in her chair, crossing her arms.

"Me?" What did I do? She hadn't been upset when I changed the location of our girls' night.

"Now there's a second one, and he's even hotter." Her lips turned down into a pout.

I shifted so I could peer through the open doorway without being obvious and assessed the guy standing in Dylan's kitchen drinking a beer. Yeah. He was good-looking. I had to give Savannah that, but in no world would I say he was hotter. The guy was tall, but Dylan had at least two inches on him. And although they were both fit, Dylan had a leaner, more defined build.

I locked eyes with Dylan, only then realizing I'd been caught checking him out. His mouth lifted into a smirk that made my cheeks flush all over again. Quickly, I turned back to the girls.

Savannah was sitting ramrod straight in her seat, grinning and beckoning the guys out here with one finger.

"What are you doing?" I whisper-yelled.

"Getting an introduction."

Head dropped back, I groaned. Why had I thought this was a good idea?

Dylan appeared with his friend on his heels. "Did you need something?"

"Yes." Savannah ran her tongue along her bottom lip seductively.

Irritation flared inside me. Jesus. How was I even related to her? If our parents one day told us that she had been adopted, I doubted any of us would be surprised.

Savannah nodded at the mystery man. "Wanted you to introduce me to your friend."

Funny how she didn't say *us*.

"I would love to." Dylan broke into a Cheshire smile, his eyes twinkling with mischief.

What was he up to?

"This is Logan." Dylan thumbed over at the guy, then pointed to my sister. "And this is Savannah."

She scooted over and patted the spot beside her. "Come sit, Logan."

Eyes widening, Logan glanced over at Dylan, who only smirked.

"Come on, I promise I don't bite." She puckered her lips into a pout. "Unless you're into that, then I totally bite."

The whole room erupted into groans at her shameless flirting.

"Do the rest of us not get an introduction?" I still didn't understand why Dylan hadn't introduced the rest of the group yet. There were very few people I was comfortable enough with to call out, and Dylan was slowly starting to fall into that category.

"No," Savannah and Dylan said at the same time.

I narrowed my eyes at him. Why was he being rude?

He just shrugged. "The last thing you need right now is to be dating someone. Especially a single dad."

My sister groaned. "Damn. Why are all the good ones taken, gay, or dads?"

"Savannah," I scolded, even though Logan chuckled at her saltiness.

She shrugged. "I'm not really mom material. You know that."

I rolled my eyes. That was a lie. She used it to keep from having to grow up and settle down. A classic case of Peter Pan syndrome.

I spun in my seat and shot Dylan a glare. "I didn't mean to date. I meant you should be polite and introduce all of us, since Savannah isn't the only one sitting here."

He crossed his arms, cocking an eyebrow.

"I already know Logan," Cece chirped. "Sarah does too."

Although Sarah had stayed home with her daughter, who wasn't feeling well, Cece had left her baby home with Owen.

Savannah perked up. "Wait, is he one of your dad's hot fire-fighters?"

Cece's eyes popped wide. "Umm, he *is* one of the firefight-ers. Not commenting on the hot part."

Dylan tipped his head in my direction. "That's Hattie Williams. You know her brother Kyle."

Logan nodded. "I thought you looked familiar."

I smiled and waved. My brother was a paramedic and had been working at Half Moon Lake FD for over a year now. He'd dealt with some demons after being discharged from the mili-tary, but he'd eventually found not only a passion, but also his wife Tina and her kids.

Once Dylan had introduced Brittney, Rachel, and Kelly, we fell into easy conversation. Savannah, of course, continued to shamelessly flirt with Logan throughout the evening.

Hmm. Did this mean she'd break her no dating dads rule?

Feeling the weight of a gaze, I scanned the group, eventually finding Dylan watching me. I shifted uncomfortably and glanced away. The intensity with which he studied me was palpable. It was strange, to be under such scrutiny. Sure, if I were in distress, my family and friends would pick up on it, but more often than not, I had no trouble quietly sneaking away without garnering any attention. Not with Dylan, though. Every time I moved, his gaze would zero in on me again.

After another round of margaritas, Savannah bounced in her seat. "Let's play Put a Finger Down."

I groaned. "We're not sixteen anymore."

"Don't even." She shot daggers at me. "We played this last summer, and you weren't complaining then."

"I was drunk and figured it was easier to just go along with it."

"Perfect." With a smirk, she held her hand up, fingers splayed. "Go along with it this time too."

The girls all followed suit. The men did not.

Savannah raised a brow at Logan.

"I'm too old for this." He shook his head.

Dylan sat back in his seat and crossed his arms. He obviously thought this was stupid too.

"Age is just a number." My sister scoffed. "But whatever. Okay. Put a finger down if you've had sex in the last three months."

Of all the women here, I was the only one who didn't put a finger down. Shit. Grinning, Brittney elbowed me, and heat flooded my face. God, I hated my sister right now.

We went around the circle, each naming a Put a Finger Down question. I had two fingers left.

"Put a finger down," Cece said, "if you've ever had a one-night stand."

And again, I was the only one in the group who'd never had that experience. One more round, and it was Savannah's turn again.

"Put a finger down if you've ever wanted to bang one of your brother's best friends." She smirked at me as she put another finger down.

Jesus. Why did she insist on making me want to punch her? I put my hand down, officially done with this stupid game.

But I immediately wished I hadn't when Savannah waggled her brows in Dylan's direction and mouthed *so what are you going to do about that?*

"Savannah," Brittney scolded.

I glared at my sister, refusing to look over at Dylan, even though I could feel his gaze on me.

"On that note," Cece said as she stood. "It's late. We should probably call it a night."

"Yeah, I think my sister has had enough of me for one night." Savannah bounced to her feet, grinning.

"Yep." I sent her a smile that clearly conveyed my desire to strangle her.

We cleaned up, taking our glasses into the kitchen, and one by one, the girls headed out, with Logan leaving a minute later. I was exhausted but figured I should clean up a bit since Dylan had so generously offered his house for our gathering. Barely keeping my eyes open, I loaded the glasses into the dishwasher. As I turned away from the counter, that sensation hit me again. His eyes were on me. A shiver raced down my spine as I spun to face him.

"You look tired. You should head to bed."

The spark of excitement morphed into annoyance instantly. Of course he'd have to open his mouth and remind me that he was a bossy asshole.

I held back an eye roll. "Yes, Dad."

He smirked and turned back to his computer. "Just an observation."

"Aren't you coming to bed too?"

His spine visibly stiffened.

My stomach twisted as I replayed the words in my head. Oh god. "I-I mean," I sputtered, "are you going to bed? Like are you not heading to bed yourself?" There, that was much better. Not awkward or weird.

"Yeah, in a bit. Want to go through some of these names first." He kept his focus fixed on his computer.

"Okay." I shrugged. "Good night."

"Night."

I'd made it up three steps before a muttered curse from Dylan had me freezing. The legs of his chair scraped across the floor, then his low voice rumbled through the room and up the stairs.

"How the hell did he get near her apartment again without being seen?"

My heart lurched. I turned around, wishing I could hear the other side of the conversation. Was he talking about my apartment? Maybe not. Not everything was about me. He was probably working on other cases.

"No, she went to bed. She can't hear me." The second the words were out of his mouth, he turned and spotted me where I was hovering on the staircase. His shoulders fell. "Aiden, let me call you back."

"What happened?" I scurried back down to the kitchen, my heart in my throat.

He pinched the bridge of his nose. "He spray-painted *slut* on your apartment door."

Wow. Clearly Dylan couldn't sugarcoat a thing, even if he tried. Though I guess I couldn't blame him for going with the rip-the-Band-Aid off approach.

"How?" I blinked, trying to find better words, but they escaped me.

He shrugged. "That's what I was trying to find out. My guess is that Aiden had someone driving by, but not actively checking the apartment."

I balled my hands into fists at my side, hating all of it. Not only the fear of someone watching me, but everyone else who had to watch me too. Having police circling my apartment, needing a babysitter. It was like, in one fell swoop, this stalker had taken away all my privacy. But the only way to stop it was to let Dylan and Aiden do their jobs.

I nodded. "Okay." This wasn't going to end until this psycho was caught.

"Hattie..." Dylan started.

I raised a hand. "I'm fine." Or I was going to make myself be.

He scoffed. "Fine never means fine."

With a shrug, I turned and made my way upstairs without looking back. Fine was all I could give him right now. Though if I was being honest, none of this was fine.

He knew it too.

I wish I could say that the moment my head hit the pillow, I was passed out, but for a long time after I crawled into bed, my thoughts continued to whirl. I cycled between the fear of how easily this guy was getting around the police and to my apartment and the frustration that because he could do that, I wasn't even allowed to be home.

I closed my eyes, praying sleep would come.

I stood in an open field without a single familiar landmark. Was I dreaming?

A figure cloaked in black approached me, calling out my name, beckoning me to him. No. He wouldn't get me. I would fight. Turning, I sprinted into the dark woods, running as fast as I could but feeling like the ground under me was moving in the opposite direction.

Feeling as though I was getting nowhere, I glanced over my shoulder to find that the faceless man was closing in quickly. As I turned, determined to pick up my pace, he grabbed my arm.

I pushed and pushed against him, flinging my arms to loosen his grasp and screaming out for help.

Finally, Dylan's voice broke through the darkness.

Relief washed over me. Dylan was here. He'd save me.

"Hattie, wake up. Need you to wake up."

Startling, I opened my eyes. With shaky breaths, I blinked the scene in front of me into focus. Dylan. He was hovering above me, his lips turned down in a concerned frown.

"If I let go, will you promise not to punch me again?"

Only then did I realize that he had my arms pinned to the mattress on either side of me.

I nodded. Had I actually hit him?

The small lamp on the nightstand was on, but the room was still cast in shadows. With a sigh, he let go of my wrists and sat on the edge of the bed.

"I punched you?" I raised up on one elbow, scanning his face to make sure I hadn't really hurt him. The guy had enough to deal with already. He didn't need a fat lip or a black eye too.

He smirked, his face looking unscathed and perfect as always. "Yeah, and I'm pretty sure you enjoyed it."

"You *can* be a bossy ass." Although I had to admit, his assertiveness was comforting at times.

"Remind me to thank Kyle or Rhett the next time I see them."

I tilted my head. "Why?"

"For teaching you how to throw a mean right hook." He rubbed the left side of his jaw. Drama king. It didn't even look red. "Want a cup of tea or warm milk?"

I grimaced. "I never understood the warm milk thing. It's disgusting."

He shrugged. "I prefer whiskey."

"That sounds good."

"I make a decent hot toddy. Want one?"

"Sure." I sat up and let the sheet drop to my waist.

Rather than standing and heading to the kitchen, he remained frozen, his gaze zeroing in on my chest. I glanced down and cursed. Once again, I was wearing a thin tank and no bra. I yanked the sheet back up and let out a huff.

He stood abruptly and turned toward the door. "I'll meet you downstairs."

Then he was gone, and I fell back against my pillow, struggling to find my breath again.

Chapter Thirteen

DYLAN

WHY WAS I making hot toddies at one in the morning? The last thing I needed was whiskey. But then again, maybe that was exactly what I needed. Along with a reminder that my job was to protect her. Not to ogle her the way I had upstairs when her nipples were poking through her thin tank top.

Jesus. I needed to get my head on straight. It was much easier to push aside my attraction to her before I knew it was two-sided. But the way her skin flushed when Savannah asked that last question confirmed it. Had the shit-stirring sibling been this relentless when Jackson and Ashley were fighting their attraction to each other?

Footsteps sounded on the stairs, and a moment later, she padded into the kitchen behind me.

"Here." I turned and handed her one warm mug.

Our fingers brushed as she took it from me. The sensation did nothing to quiet the need coursing through me. At least she had a sweatshirt on.

"Thanks." Head tilted to the side, she smiled.

I nodded. "You're welcome."

"Sorry I woke you."

"You didn't." I was so engrossed with my search into possible suspects that I hadn't realized how late it was. Then I'd gotten sucked into an episode of *Perfect Wife*. "I was watching TV."

I left it at that. No use getting her worked up about the stalker situation again.

"Oh." She brought the cup of warm whiskey to her lips and took a sip. "What were you watching?"

"A true crime documentary."

Her nose wrinkled in the cutest way. "You watch that crap?"

Agitation stirred in my gut. My ex used to complain about how dumb those kinds of shows were. She would never watch them, and any time I tried, she would make snide comments. I supposed I shouldn't be surprised that Hattie had a similar opinion.

"It's like an addiction." I shrugged. "If it's on, I get sucked in."

There was a pull there. To solve the mystery.

She chuckled. "That's how I am with *The Kardashians*."

A scoff escaped me before I could stop it. "That's worse."

She rolled her eyes. "That's debatable. At least mine's entertaining."

I slipped my free hand into the pocket of my sweats. "If you say so."

"Want to put one on while we drink our whiskey?"

"*The Kardashians*?"

"No." She giggled, "True crime. Might bore me enough to lull me back to sleep." With a smirk, she spun, and my eyes locked on to her ass. Round and perfect, and the bottom of each cheek played a game of peek-a-boo with the hem of her almost nonexistent shorts.

I stood in the middle of the kitchen for several heartbeats, just staring at her, before I forced my feet to move. When we were settled side by side on the sofa, I cued up the episode that I'd started upstairs and turned the volume down a bit, assuming she'd prefer a little background noise over actually focusing on the show. But ten minutes in, she was asking questions and trying to understand the case and its details.

"It was the husband. It's always the husband."

I shook my head but kept my mouth shut. She obviously wasn't familiar with the real news story and its outcome.

"Really? It's not the husband?"

"I don't want to give it away."

With a huff, she turned back to the TV, pulled her legs up under her, and took another sip of her drink. The movement caused her to lean closer, and as the smell of fresh rain hit me, I breathed in deep.

After the episode had ended, she shifted a little closer. "Do they find the women who kidnapped her?"

Our thighs brushed, sending a spark of electricity through me. Swallowing, I worked to recall her question.

I blinked. "Want to watch the next episode and find out?"

"Sure." She leaned forward to grab the remote from the coffee table, her long hair brushing my forearm.

I should scoot away, but being in her space, breathing in the smell of fresh rain, was intoxicating.

"I'm still not tired, and now I want to know what happens."

I leaned back and settled in deeper. She followed suit, slumping against the back of the couch and almost into the crook of my arm.

"I thought it was going to bore you to sleep."

"Shut up and push play." Smirking, she held the remote out to me.

This time, she only made it about halfway through the episode before her head drooped, landing on my shoulder, and let out a tiny, adorable snore.

I let her stay there, not wanting to wake her. It felt good, so fucking good, and it was innocent enough. After the things Savannah had said tonight, I couldn't stop thinking about what it would be like to be with Hattie. Hold her like this any time I wanted. Kiss her, touch her.

But none of that mattered. I'd never know. She was my best friend's sister and the woman I had been charged with protecting.

I slid out from under her, easing her down so she was lying on her side, then covered her with a blanket. I didn't want to risk waking her, but I also couldn't leave her down here by herself.

So it looked like I was sleeping on the couch for the second night in a row.

Chapter Fourteen

HATTIE

Yesterday had been blessedly quiet. Today too. No flowers or creepy texts. The only weirdness I'd been experiencing came from staying at Dylan's. Probably because I'd known him for what felt like forever. Domestic tasks like going to the grocery store and cooking dinner together were strangely comfortable. We actually made a good team and liked a lot of the same food, so it came naturally.

Now, I stepped behind the bar at The Dock to retrieve the envelope of cash that needed to be dropped off at the bank.

Suddenly feeling eyes on me, I looked up and scanned the restaurant. It only took a moment to find Dylan, who was watching me while he chatted with Jamie at the hostess stand.

"Did you get more flowers?" a male voiced asked from behind me.

Heart lurching, I spun, finding Michael and his two friends sitting at the bar. "What?"

"Oh yeah, I forgot about that." Michael nudged Paul, and they both snickered. "Did your cop boyfriend send you more flowers yet?"

The regulars around here really needed to get their own lives. How they sat here every day for hours and drank was beyond me. I opened my mouth to respond, but before I could, Dylan stepped up beside me and placed his arm around my waist.

"Nah. I opted to make dinner for her at my place yesterday instead."

I held my breath and peered up at him. What the hell was he doing? That statement definitely implied something that wasn't anywhere near the truth.

"You ready?" he murmured, bringing his head closer to mine. "Better get going if we're going to make it to the bank before they close."

Crap. Right. And I hadn't driven today. Dylan had insisted on dropping me off on his way to work.

"Need to get my bag."

"Okay." He released me, then lifted his chin, turning toward Paul and Josh. "You guys are fairly new to town, right?"

Paul nodded and launched into a monologue about how much he loved it here and planned to stay indefinitely.

I remained where I was for a minute, noticing that although Dylan's questions were casual, he was actually subtly digging for information. None of them batted an eye as they spilled all kinds of details about themselves. Of all the people to grill, he'd chosen the three drunks? Did he really think they were capable of anything but drinking and being obnoxious? He better not scare them off. Rhett would lose it. We stocked some of our best beer each week just for these guys.

After a moment, I excused myself and headed toward my offices, and when I came back out, he was still talking with them.

"So you guys are working on the construction of the new hospital wing?" Dylan leaned his forearm on the bar, appearing genuinely interested.

"Yeah, we finished framing it all in last week." Paul turned slightly to look at me as I approached.

"I'm ready."

"Okay, babe. Let's go." Dylan smiled.

Babe? What in the ever-loving fruitcake had gotten into him?

With a hand on the small of my back, he turned me slightly, then addressed the men again. "Have a good night."

Once we were sitting side by side in his car, I pinned him with a look.

"Want to fill me in?"

He frowned like he had no clue what I was talking about. That didn't work on me. I had four siblings who'd all tried to play stupid at one point or another.

"Why did you imply we're dating?"

"Oh." He chuckled. "It wouldn't hurt to let people around here think you're dating a cop. I would rather the stalker think that than know that we're together all the time because I'm only protecting you."

Right. I guess that made sense. "Okay, but why were you pestering them with questions?"

"It's my job." He glanced over at me as he pulled out of the parking lot. "Have you dated any of those guys?"

"What? Ew, no." I cringed. Michael was probably twenty

years older than me, and although some people would love that idea, I didn't. Plus he spent every day at the bar drinking. I definitely wouldn't categorize him as a catch. "I've known Michael since I was ten."

"How about the other two?"

I found the idea of dating any of them just as disgusting for all the same reasons. "No. Gross."

He cocked a brow. "You didn't seem to be picky with the guys you met online."

Anger flared in my chest. "Don't judge. You have to cast a wide net to catch a fish."

"And all the guys from the dating sites?"

I shrugged. Online dating hadn't worked out like I wanted it to. "They were all guppies."

His lips curled up as he headed for the bank. "Okay, fine. How long have you known Michael's friends, then?"

"A few years, I guess."

"Really? Josh said he moved here early last year, and Paul said he moved here a few months ago. When he got hired to work on the hospital construction."

Huh. Felt like longer than that. Eyes squinted, I thought back, searching for my earliest memories of them. "That can't be right. I remember all three of them coming in together over the summer."

"Yeah. Paul said he visited Michael a couple of times a year until Michael got him the job three months ago."

A chime sounded through the car, indicating that Dylan had a new text from Aiden. Dylan tapped the notification on the screen, and a robotic voice read the message out loud.

"The company that sells the rare blue lady orchids is sending us a list of buyers. So far, they haven't asked for a warrant, but we'll see."

Confused, I tilted my head and studied Dylan. "Blue lady orchids?"

"Yeah. One of our techs looked into the orchids left at your place. They're rare and native to Australia. The only company we've found that sells them is there."

Australia? "So what does that mean?"

"It means that if someone on that list is local, the information will be a huge help."

I stared out the window, digesting the information. Why would someone go through so much trouble to get such a rare type of flower for me? I didn't think they were that uncommon. I swore I'd seen them before.

"Aren't blue orchids sold in most flower shops?"

He shook his head. "I wondered the same thing at first. Turns out that the blue orchids sold here in the US are dyed, not naturally blue. The blue lady orchid is naturally blue."

"You know all this?"

He didn't seem like the type to have a hidden passion for flowers, but maybe I'd misjudged him.

His laugh echoed through the car. "Nope. Violet explained all of this to Aiden and me this morning."

I pressed my lips together and racked my brain for a woman with that name. I knew just about everyone in Half Moon Lake. Or so I'd thought. "Violet?"

"Our tech. She's impressive. Finds the wildest things."

Oh. I was pretty sure I knew who he was talking about. She was fairly new to town. "Blond hair with black highlights?"

Or was it the opposite? Did she have naturally black hair with blond highlights?

"Yeah. Has a bit of that goth look to her."

"I think it's called hipster goth now."

He cocked an eyebrow. "What?"

"It's like a cool, modern goth look."

"Huh." He shrugged. "What do you want for dinner?"

On cue, my stomach growled. "Do you like sushi?"

"Love it. We can stop by Asian Palace on the way home and pick up carryout."

"Can we finish *Perfect Wife* while we eat?"

Chuckling, he twisted his hands on the wheel, making the leather creak. "Sure. Told you you'd be hooked."

"Intrigued, yes. Not hooked."

"If you say so."

After stopping by the bank, we picked up our to-go order from the sushi place, and as we stepped out onto the sidewalk, Dylan yanked me back and pressed me to his side, his arm tightly around my shoulders.

Heart racing, I glanced around, looking for the danger he must have sensed, but nothing stood out to me. His protectiveness was comforting, and his touch heated me from the inside.

Did he feel the same thing from my touch?

I relaxed against him, hoping he did. "What are you doing?" The words came out breathier than I intended as I stole a glance up at him.

He looked one way, then the other, taking in the people milling about on Main Street. "My job," he whispered as he slowly led me to his car with his arm still secured around me.

Right. This *was* his job. And I was his friend's sister. He was protecting me from a stalker. Nothing more.

It didn't matter that his embrace caused butterflies to riot in my stomach. My body needed to shut the hell up. Nothing would ever happen between the bossy detective and me.

Chapter Fifteen

DYLAN

I POURED myself a cup of coffee and leaned back against my kitchen counter, waiting on Hattie. Though she'd only been here for a couple of days, we'd already fallen into a routine. For the last three nights, we'd eaten while we chatted and then moved into the living room to watch a true crime documentary. For someone who claimed she didn't like that type of show, she was as enthusiastic as I was about figuring out the mystery.

I checked my watch, wondering if I could predict the exact time she'd appear. I appreciated routines, although I never could obtain that with Becca. We had lived together for almost a year, yet I never could get a handle on what to expect and when. She swung from sweet to passive aggressive quickly, making it impossible to keep up with or anticipate her moods. Yet it had taken only a few days to figure Hattie out.

Until now.

When she appeared, still in her tiny sleep shorts and an oversized sweatshirt, unease settled in my gut.

"Why aren't you ready?"

She looked down, her face expressionless. That look only made the disquiet inside me more acute. Had she not realized that she was still in her pajamas? I didn't think that was plausible. Sure, she was a bit unaware at times, but not in a chaotic sort of way.

The desire to snatch the phone out of her hand and demand she tell me what was wrong pulsed violently in my chest. She'd done the same thing for three mornings in a row. She'd get up, take a shower, get dressed, and then come down for coffee before going back up to do her hair and makeup. Yet today, she'd completely deviated from that routine.

Maybe I'd been wrong about her. Maybe Hattie really was unpredictable like Becca.

She looked up at me, her expression a mix of confusion and fear. "I thought...I mean...How..."

I set my coffee on the counter and closed the space between us. "What's wrong?"

She blew out a shaky breath. "He texted me."

"Who?"

"The stalker." She tucked her chin to her chest and studied her phone, then looked back up at me again.

A wave of relief rushed through me. This was exactly what I had been hoping for. He knew she'd blocked him, or at least assumed it. That meant he was watching her closely.

"That's good."

"Good?" Her eyes widened. "I don't understand. How is that a good thing? Didn't you block him?"

I nodded. "I blocked the original number. If he sent you another text, that means he bought a new burner."

Gently, I pried the phone from her hand. I needed to get this new number over to Aiden. Hopefully the burner phone had been purchased at the same gas station and we could get the surveillance recording.

"You and I obviously have different understandings of what *good* means." She sounded defeated, and her whole body sagged as she sat on one of the stools at the island.

I read the text he'd sent, cursing under my breath. Damn, no wonder she was so upset.

> He'll never have you. You are mine. Soon, you'll see that.

Although that message was not ideal, it did mean that my plan was working. Word that Hattie and I were dating had gotten around. Now we were aware that the stalker knew it too.

"I'm staying home today," she said, gaze focused on the granite in front of her.

"I don't think—"

She lifted her head and hit me with a pleading look so pitiful I knew I'd give her anything she asked for in that moment. I stepped in close and gripped her shoulder. At the mix of dejection and fear in her expression, I pulled her up and into my chest. "Okay. I'll let Aiden know that I won't be in."

"You don't have to—"

"If you're about to suggest I leave you here by yourself today—"

"Right. No. That's probably not a good idea either."

My stomach twisted painfully. "It's fine, Hattie. I can work from home."

"You sure?"

Was I sure? Mostly. Regardless, I'd say what I needed to in order to convince her that it was fine. If staying home today would make her feel better, then that was what we'd do.

"Yeah. I can even find another true crime documentary to bore you with if you want." I sent her a wink.

For the first time since stepping into the kitchen five minutes ago, she cracked a smile. "Or...I can introduce you to the world of *The Kardashians*."

I cringed at the tortuous idea but responded with, "Sure."

Whatever it took to make her smile and forget about the stalker who'd just threatened her.

HATTIE

I HAD to give Dylan credit. He made it through one whole episode of *The Kardashians*. I half expected him to get up and leave the room within minutes, but not only did he stick out the entire episode, I even caught him chuckling a couple of times.

Fresh bowl of popcorn in hand, I shuffled back to the living room. "That wasn't too bad, was it?" I sat on the sofa across from him.

One corner of his mouth lifted into a smirk. "Depends on what your definition of bad is."

Amusement threaded through me. "Come on, admit it. You laughed."

"Yeah, the way you would laugh at someone who trips and falls." He shrugged and went back to working on his computer.

I picked up the remote to play another episode and popped a kernel of popcorn into my mouth.

"Where did you find the popcorn?" His brows pulled together.

Frowning, I assessed him. "In your cabinet..."

"Interesting."

Interesting? Wasn't that where most people kept their popcorn? In their cabinets or pantries? "Huh?"

"I don't buy popcorn anymore."

Confused, I tilted my head, working through that strange choice of words. *Anymore* would imply he used to.

"Becca, my ex, liked it."

This was the first time he'd mentioned his ex to me, and now I was curious. She'd come to Ashley and Jackson's wedding with Dylan last year. She was beautiful, with long red hair. I had thought they made a cute couple.

"Do you want some?" I asked, extending the bowl across the coffee table toward him.

"No." He put his hand up. "I'm good."

"You don't like popcorn?"

He chuckled, focus cast on his computer again. "Who doesn't like popcorn?"

"I went out with a guy once—to a movie—and he gave me a solid five-minute lecture before the previews started about how bad the popcorn I was eating was. He went on and on about the butter and salt and sodium. Then he turned on my Cherry Coke and gummy bears." I obviously didn't have a second date with him. I live to eat, I don't eat to live, and I had no interest in being judged for that. "But now that I say that, I understand why you don't want popcorn."

His head snapped up. "What does that mean?"

"Look at you. There isn't an ounce of fat on your body as far as I can see, so it's safe to assume you have a pretty strict diet."

He shrugged. "Nah. I try to stick to healthy food, but I prefer salty foods over sweet. So chips and popcorn are my go-to snacks rather than ice cream and candy. I don't really do fast food, though."

With that, he turned his attention back to his work, so I pushed play. I tried to focus on the conversation between Kim and Kourtney, but quickly, my curiosity got the better of me. I pressed pause and shifted to look at him again.

"So what happened?"

He peered at me over his computer and cocked his head to the side. "What happened with what?"

"Becca." What else would I be talking about?

Sighing, he leaned forward and set his laptop on the coffee table.

Guilt flashed through me. "I'm sorry. I know you're trying to work. I'll stop talking."

"It's fine." He rubbed a hand over the back of his neck. "Probably should break for lunch soon anyway."

"Lunch?" I glanced over at the time displayed on the smart speaker that sat on top of the fireplace mantel. "It's only eleven o'clock."

"You don't eat breakfast, so I guess I assumed that you liked to eat lunch early."

"I have popcorn." I held up the bowl. "But yeah, typically, I eat lunch before noon because I'm not a big breakfast person."

"I've noticed." He smirked.

The way Dylan noticed every detail warmed my stomach. I doubted my siblings even realized that I wasn't a fan of breakfast, yet Dylan did after five days. It was hard to imagine that

116

someone who paid that much attention to detail struggled with a relationship.

"So what happened with Becca?"

Lips pressed together, he sat back. "She struggled to accept my job."

From the defeat in his tone, there was more to it than that. What he just said was akin to *we parted ways amicably*.

"Like the danger? Was she afraid that something might happen to you?"

He tensed, his expression shuttering. "I'm not really sure."

A niggle of guilt itched at the back of my brain. Crap. I was a jerk for bringing up his ex.

"A lot of it was the unpredictability of my schedule. It was a problem before we moved in together, and I thought living in the same place would help. Instead, it kind of made things worse."

"How?" I set the bowl of popcorn on the table and leaned forward, my hands clasped in my lap.

"She felt like I was never there for her when she wanted me to be. Then, when she felt like I'd let her down, she would spend days or even weeks mad at me about it."

I frowned. That sounded toxic.

"No matter what I did, it wasn't enough, and eventually, I stopped trying. It took a long time to realize how unhealthy our relationship had gotten. But once I did, I ended it."

I nodded, although I couldn't relate. The last semiserious relationship I'd been in was during college over five years ago, and that had just fizzled out. It wasn't toxic or dramatic, but it wasn't passionate either.

"Are we starting another one?" He nodded at the TV. "Or breaking for lunch?"

I glanced down at the bowl of popcorn. "Let's watch one more before we eat."

With a cleansing breath, I pressed play.

A minute later, I felt his eyes still on me, but when I looked back over, he was focused on his computer screen once again.

Chapter Sixteen

HATTIE

Thursday 8:40 p.m.

UNKNOWN:

Why aren't you talking to me?

Friday 5:48 p.m.

UNKNOWN:

I'm going to have to scrub his touch from
your body.

Saturday 11:12 a.m.

UNKNOWN:

You look so beautiful with your hair curled
like that.

Chapter Seventeen

HATTIE

Saturday 6:22 p.m.
All the single ladies

Savannah: It's been a week, so what's the verdict?

Me: Verdict is this guy keeps texting me every day, and it's freaking me out.

Brittney: Ah, shit. Really? Have you not blocked the new number?

Me: Not yet. Dylan wants to keep the information coming in. See if he says something that gives anything away.

Savannah: I mean, that sucks, but it's not what I was talking about.

Rachel: Savannah strikes again. We can always count on you to jump into the chat with some random statement or question you expect us all to understand.

Savannah: No one else has been wondering if our Hattie has found out what the sexy detective is packing?

Brittney: No.

Cece: Nope.

Rachel: Maybe a little.

Me: I already told you I'm not sleeping with Rhett's friend.

Savannah: I saw you together at The Dock earlier this week. I'm calling bullshit.

Me: GIF of a woman rolling her eyes

Me: What's with you lately?

Savannah: Don't get me started.

Rachel: She's going through a dry spell 🙄

Me: Wait, what?

Kelly: GIF of a woman shocked

Cece: GIF of a woman screaming NOOO!

Sarah: GIF of sad dog eyes

> Me: Sorry, there will be no living vicariously through me.

Savannah: GIF saying that's bullshit

Chapter Eighteen

HATTIE

TAKING Dylan Gray to Sunday family dinner had never crossed my mind before this week. He'd been to plenty of parties at our house over the years, but never one of these. Sunday dinner was just that. A time for my family to gather. My siblings brought their spouses and kids. If one of us was dating someone seriously, we might bring them as well. I hadn't brought someone in over five years.

My parents and siblings knew why Dylan was coming with me, but still, it felt weird.

Not as weird, though, as how well he fit in.

Maybe it shouldn't have been strange. Maybe I shouldn't have been surprised. I supposed it made sense, since he'd been friends with Rhett and Jackson for more than a decade.

"How's the case coming?"

I paused with my fork halfway to my mouth and looked up at Kyle, who was sitting across the table. Was he asking me or Dylan? I glanced sideways at Dylan before meeting my brother's gaze again.

Kyle tilted his head. "Something else happen?"

Setting my fork down, I cleared my throat. "The stalker is texting me again, but Dylan say's that's a good thing."

Kyle shot Dylan a glare I couldn't decipher. Was it because, like me, he didn't understand how being threatened like that could possibly be positive?

Though I was struggling to comprehend the way Dylan saw things, I believed him, and I trusted him to know what was best. So I shrugged. "He says that means the stalker bought another burner phone, so this time, they might get him on tape."

Beside me, Dylan let out a sigh and sat back in his chair, crossing his arms over his chest.

Kyle continued to glare, and Dylan looked like he was about to ask him what his problem was. My stomach sank. Great, a pissing contest between the two bossy, controlling men.

"That is good," Rhett interjected, glancing over at Kyle. "Isn't it?" Leave it to him to miss the tense vibes around the table.

"Depends," Kyle said. "Do you have anything to show for it yet?"

"He paid cash for both burners, including the minutes and data." Dylan locked his jaw, his eyes narrowing. "And the place where he picked up the second burner doesn't have surveillance cameras."

Heart thumping against my sternum, I whipped around and blinked at Dylan. This was the first time I was hearing this.

"So it's not actually a good thing after all, is it? If it hasn't amounted to anything," Kyle bit out.

Wow, he was in rare form tonight.

"Dylan and Aiden are the best," Rhett said. "I trust that they will figure this out. You need to chill, man."

I had to agree with my idiot brother this time. Kyle really did need to chill. I understood why he was annoyed, but Dylan and Aiden were doing the best they could. Kyle knew our small-town police department didn't deal with these types of things on a regular basis and had little in the way of resources to do much more than handle traffic citations and the occasional break-in or petty theft. What did he expect?

Thankfully, Bella jumped in then and shifted the topic to Tina and her impending due date, asking whether she was ready for the new baby.

"Yes and no." She placed her hand gingerly on the top of her large belly. "I'm ready to meet her, but I'm going to miss being pregnant."

Her due date was only weeks away, and given that this was her third child, her doctor told her she might go into labor earlier than she had with the first two.

Bella chuckled. "I *do not* miss being pregnant."

"I thought you wanted one more?" Ashley narrowed her eyes at her best friend.

"We do. But that doesn't mean I enjoy being pregnant." Bella shrugged.

As if on cue, Hudson began crying from the living room.

"Finish your food." Rhett stood and nodded to Bella's plate. "I got him."

I tracked him as he disappeared through the large archway that led into the living room. My mom had set up a card table in there for the kids while the adults sat at the dining room table.

I smiled. She might need a bigger table for the kids soon. Between Rhett and Bella's two, Kyle and Tina's two and a third on the way, and Sophia, who had been officially adopted by Jackson and Ashley, the kids' table was getting full.

Dylan leaned over my shoulder and reached for my empty plate, his proximity causing my skin to tingle. He froze and locked eyes with me. That look went straight to my core.

Dammit. Once again, my body was reacting to him without my brain's permission.

Standing to his full height, he smirked like he knew exactly how he affected me. I squared my shoulders and picked up a few plates, then followed him into the kitchen.

After dinner had been cleaned up, the guys hunkered down in the living room with the kids and the women stood around the kitchen, having various types of alcoholic and nonalcoholic after-dinner drinks.

"This was so nice." My mother brought her glass of wine to her lips and took a sip. "Dylan fits right in with everyone."

"He's been friends with Rhett and Jackson forever. Of course he fit in." I sat beside Bella at the island with my own wineglass in hand.

"I'm not coming anymore." Savannah huffed as she leaned back against one of the marble countertops. Surprisingly she opted for a cup of piping-hot coffee rather than alcohol. "Everyone's coupled up."

"I'm not even dating anyone," I reminded her.

She was always dramatic, but tonight, it was over-the-top.

"Yet." She smirked. "Give it another week, and that'll change."

I rolled my eyes. *Here we go again.*

"Wait..." Bella started. "You and Dylan?"

"No." I shook my head. "Savannah's just trying to stir up trouble."

"I think you two would make a cute couple." Ashley chuckled. "Although I hope Rhett takes the news better than he did when he found out I was dating Jackson."

"Guess we'll never know, since I have no intention of dating Dylan." I sighed.

God, my family was exhausting.

"If he finds out another one of his friends is dating one of his sisters, he'll definitely lose his mind," Bella said.

Had no one heard me? Or were they choosing to ignore what I'd said? Maybe I was attracted to him, that I could admit, but he was doing his job while also doing a favor for his best friend.

Whatever. It would be a waste of breath to try to convince them they were wrong.

Though maybe I could use a little convincing myself.

Even my own mother, who wasn't prone to dramatics, was sending me a smirk like she agreed with my sisters.

Chapter Nineteen

DYLAN

"SORRY ABOUT KYLE." Hattie shifted in her seat.

"It's fine. I get it." I slowly drove down her parents' street. "Aiden and I were pissed too when we discovered there was no camera."

"Why didn't you tell me?"

I sent a sideways glance her way before focusing back on the road again, a lump forming in my throat. "I didn't want to upset you."

She was quiet for way too long before she quietly said, "I

wouldn't have been upset. Maybe a little disappointed, but not mad or anything like that."

I nodded. Yeah, I figured that out after the news was out. Before tonight, I'd assumed she would be pissed when she discovered that the texts from her stalker had gotten us nowhere so far. It had also dawned on me that maybe the issues Becca and I had were still messing with me.

Hattie and I weren't together, but she was the first woman that I had spent significant time with since the end of that relationship.

"You don't need to keep things from me. I'm a big girl. I can handle it."

It had nothing to do with thinking she couldn't handle it. But was I really going to admit the truth?

"It wasn't that." I gripped the steering wheel a little tighter. "Honestly, I assumed you would be mad at me."

"What? Why?" Mouth turned down, she studied me in the light from the streetlamps we passed. "Did you know he was going to buy the new burner at a place without cameras?"

"Well, no. But—"

"It could have led to something, but it didn't." She sighed. "It is what it is, and there's nothing we can do about it, so why stress?"

I didn't know what to say. Of course she was right. But with Becca, it never mattered whether the issue was within my control. If I requested time off or tried to switch with another officer and it didn't work out, it was my fault.

Her phone chimed where it sat on her lap, and she picked it up, swiping her thumb up the screen to unlock it.

"Jesus," she huffed.

"What's wrong?"

"Just this creep sending me yet another freaking text. I get that he's unhinged, but take the hint already."

I hated that this was causing her stress. And for what? It wasn't like he was giving us anything useful.

"Go ahead and block the number."

"What?" She assessed me, brows pulled together. "You said it was better not to do that. Don't let my brother change your mind."

As I came to a stop at a red light, I turned to look at her. "Doesn't have anything to do with your brother. I don't like that this guy is upsetting you."

She opened her mouth to speak, but I continued before she could.

"I know you can handle it. But I don't want you to have to if it's not necessary, and so far, he's been careful. I don't think we're going to get anything from the actual texts at this point."

"Okay." A deep sigh escaped her as she focused on her phone again. "What do you want to watch tonight? It's your turn to pick," she said once she put her phone back down in her lap.

The smile she sent me had my entire body relaxing.

"*The Kardashians* is fine."

She chuckled. "I knew it. You are totally into it, aren't you?"

I shrugged. "After tonight, something light would be good."

As we walked into the house, she made a beeline for the kitchen. I didn't even have to ask what she wanted. I grabbed a Cherry Coke out of the fridge for her while she pulled a packet of microwave popcorn from the box in the cabinet.

When I handed the bottle to her, our fingers brushed, and her breath hitched.

I hated that I noticed her reactions to my touch. That I liked it. That I wanted to know what kind of sound she'd make if I pressed my lips to her neck and then lower...

"Dylan?" she said breathlessly.

I blinked back to the present. Jesus, I needed to get my head straight. Letting go of the bottle, I stepped back. "I'll get the episode set up while you make the popcorn." I didn't wait for her response before turning and heading into the living room.

The space would do me good. I needed air that didn't smell like her. At least for a moment. But when she settled on the sofa beside me, bringing the scent of fresh rain with her, it was as if I couldn't survive without it.

We'd been sitting on opposite couches for the past several days, but that changed last night, when I'd given in to the offer of popcorn. I assumed we'd pass the bowl back and forth across the coffee table, but instead, she scampered over and set it between us on the two-person sofa.

Now I was trapped. There was no polite way to say *could you please go sit over there? You smell too damn good.*

"You okay?"

Despite the way my gut twisted, I nodded. "Yeah, why?"

"You're wearing that thinking too hard look you get sometimes."

"Just need to look up a few things." I opened my computer and forced myself to focus on it. A moment later, she picked up the remote and pressed play, and I breathed a sigh of relief.

Ten minutes into the episode, thunder rumbled in the distance. Out of the corner of my eye, I could have sworn Hattie flinched.

My phone blared where it rested on the coffee table, pulling my attention away from her. I quickly snagged it and dismissed the severe weather alert.

Luckily, I'd invested in a standby generator last year after we'd lost electricity for two days. A thunderstorm in January likely wouldn't be too bad, but if it was followed by any type of icy precipitation or came with strong winds, there was a decent chance there would be damage to power lines.

Thunder rumbled again, this time louder, and Hattie

jumped a foot in the air. Breathing audibly, she brought her legs up and tucked them under herself.

After another crack of thunder, followed by a bolt of lightning that lit up the house, she almost jumped off the couch.

"Shit." Rather than the show, her attention was glued to the large windows lining the opposite wall.

"What's wrong?" I asked, taking in her wide eyes.

She shook her head. "Nothing. I'm fine."

I wasn't buying it, and when thunder shook the house and lightning lit up the darkness outside the front windows, she practically leaped into my lap.

"Are you afraid of storms?"

"No." She squared her shoulders.

My only response was a raised eyebrow.

When the wind picked up, whistling through the trees, she pinched her eyes closed. "Okay, fine." Her shoulders sagged. "I hate thunderstorms."

It was ironic that she was afraid of thunderstorms, given that she always smelled like mountain air after a rainstorm.

"Why?"

Eyes narrowed, she huffed. "It's stupid. If I tell you, you'll probably laugh at me."

I laid my hand on her knee. "I promise I won't."

She stared at me for so long I was sure she wouldn't tell me, but when the wind howled again, she flinched, then cleared her throat.

"When I was fifteen, I got caught in a storm while I was walking home from a friend's house." She sighed. "It got bad really quickly. Ridiculously strong straight-line winds and hail. Then lightning struck a tree only twenty or thirty feet in front of me, bringing the whole thing down. I'd never run so fast in my life, and I was freaking out the whole time."

"I remember thinking you all seemed unreasonably shocked by the amount of damage that storm had done."

"What?" Her brows pulled together.

"I grew up on the coast, in Wilmington. I dealt with hurricanes and severe storms and flooding a lot, so for me, it was just another day."

I'd just moved to Half Moon Lake when that storm hit. I'd been relieved that my parents hadn't been hit, since it didn't come up the coast. The damage was mostly centralized in the mountains.

Guilt wormed its way through me at the thought of my parents. It had been too long since I'd been home to visit. I'd left for the police academy at eighteen and had moved here right after graduation, so I didn't see my parents as often as I would like. But I tried to call Mom and Dad at least once a week.

Thunder shook the house, and she let out a whimper, pulling her knees up to her chest and pressing her head to them.

I put the bowl of popcorn on the table and scooted closer, placing my hand on her back. "What can I do?"

"Nothing. I just have to ride it out," she mumbled without lifting her head.

Was this how she reacted to every thunderstorm? If so, it had to be miserable. I rubbed my hand up and down her back, feeling her jump each time the thunder shook the house. Eventually, I couldn't take it anymore and pulled her flush against my side.

A loud popping sound outside echoed through the house, and then we were sitting in total darkness.

"Dylan," she whispered, voice shaky.

"It's okay—"

She burrowed further into my side, and her scent enveloped me, short-circuiting my brain.

I cleared my throat. "I think a transformer blew. The generator should kick on in a second."

Thankfully, after Hattie took another shaky breath in, it turned on, and the living room lit up once again.

I smirked down at her. "See? All good."

Rather than relief, her face was a mask of uncertainty. Thunder and wind continued to rattle the windows. Every time, she'd whimper.

Fuck, her terror gutted me. "Stop thinking about it. Focus on something else." I wanted to tell her to focus on me, my voice, my touch. But I couldn't go there.

She shook her head. "I can't."

"Yes, you can." I ran my hand up her bare arm.

Her breath hitched at the contact, and our gazes locked. I was tempted to lean in and take her mind off the chaos happening outside.

See if her lips were as soft as they looked.

My stomach dropped. What the hell was I thinking?

It would be better, for both of us, if I got her talking. "Tell me about the weirdest date you've ever been on."

Her lips quirked with the hint of a smile. "One guy asked me if I was fertile."

My lungs seized up. Was she joking? "Seriously?"

"Yep. Apparently, his mom told him to make sure any girl he went out with could have babies, because that was what was important."

"How did you respond to that?"

"Um." Her cheeks heated. "I excused myself to the bathroom and texted him, telling him that I was sick. Then I got the hell out of there."

I chuckled, the sound causing her eyes to drift to my lips.

I should pull away. Fight this.

Too much was at stake. Giving in would be a mistake, but I was leaning forward anyway.

Thunder rumbled again, and her eyes widened.

That only encouraged me. I had no intention of letting her spiral into her fear again.

I brushed my lips softly against hers, and when she melted into me, I tilted my head, deepening the kiss. It was all-consuming. My entire body, inside and out, screamed for more. Giving in to the temptation, I pulled her close. With my fingers tangled in her hair, I devoured her mouth. But a second later, when thunder rumbled again and she stiffened in my arms, I pulled back.

Fuck. Heart racing, I wiped my mouth with the back of my hand and studied her. What the hell had I done?

Space. I needed space. Because now, all I wanted to do was dive back in.

"I better check the cameras." The excuse was lame, but if I stayed here another second, I would cross more firmly drawn lines. "Make sure they're back up and running."

She nodded, her lip caught between her teeth. "Okay."

Standing, I roughed a hand down my face. Then I headed through the kitchen and into the sunroom. Once I was alone, I grabbed the back of my neck with both hands and pinched my eyes closed.

How had that happened? Better yet, why had I let it happen? My career, her safety, and Rhett's friendship were all at stake if I crossed this line. I wanted to blame it on how gorgeous she was, but I knew better. I'd been tempted by plenty of beautiful women over the years, yet I'd never given in when there were circumstances that complicated the attraction.

So what made Hattie different?

It was so much more than my physical attraction to her that drew me in. The few times she'd been vulnerable with me, I couldn't resist offering her comfort. Like the night the car followed her, and she ended up at my house. Or when the stalker scared her with his recent text. Even tonight, with her fear of thunderstorms.

I hated to see her so scared, so distraught.

A loud banging on the front door echoed through the house, making my heart leap in my chest. Shit. I'd left my phone on the coffee table. I was such an asshole. It had to be obvious to Hattie that I wasn't checking the cameras if my phone was sitting in another room.

I made my way back toward her, trying not to make eye contact. I didn't regret kissing her, but I couldn't let it happen again. And the last thing I wanted was for her to see any type of regret on my face.

I snatched my phone off the coffee table and saw I'd missed a text and phone call from Logan.

Fuck. As I turned and headed for the front door, I pulled up my camera app so I could confirm he was the person on my front porch.

With a smirk, I swung the door open. "Let me guess," I started, taking in the two adorable girls standing in front of him. The wind and rain had let up a bit, but it was still coming down, so I gestured for them to come inside. "You're in a bind and need me to watch the kids?"

The look he shot me as they hustled into the house and out of the rain said *yes, but don't give me shit about it.*

Fat fucking chance. "If you'd hire a sitter who wasn't eighty, you'd have much more reliable childcare."

"She's not that old." He huffed. "And the storm was pretty bad."

Maybe she wasn't that old, but there was no way she was under seventy. And unless it was sunny, there was no way she'd drive anywhere.

"I wasn't even supposed to be on shift tonight, but there's a big fire down at Keller's farm. Chief asked if I could assist."

Dread tugged at my stomach. "Don't tell me arson again."

He shook his head. "I don't think so. Sounds like it was a lightning strike."

"That's good. Too many fires lately, and we don't need any more suspected arsons." I raised an eyebrow at him, circling back to the reason he was standing on my porch to begin with. "But you do need a young, reliable babysitter."

"I've already told you—I refuse to be a cliché."

His reasoning for continuing to hire the old ladies was ridiculous. The last one had failing health and only showed up half the time she was supposed to. Clearly, this one wasn't any better.

"What's a cliché?" one of his five-year-old twins asked.

I still had trouble telling them apart. But based on the pink headband in her hair, I guessed it was Alice. Nikki hated pink.

"It's when someone does something predictable," Logan said, focus still fixed on me.

"What's predictable?" Nikki asked this time.

Logan sighed. "Girls, why don't you go put a show on while I talk to Dylan?"

Shrugging, Alice skipped past me. Nikki followed her with a huff. She would be a fun teenager, I was sure of it.

"I haven't said yes yet." I smirked at my friend.

"It's only for an hour or so. Maggie should be finished up at the hospital soon."

I chuckled. "Bet that conversation went well."

Grimacing, he ducked his head. "She threatened to find and hire my next babysitter."

Their relationship was strange, but they worked hard to co-parent successfully for the girls' sake.

"You should take Jay's suggestion and hire Izzy."

Logan's eyes narrowed at me, and he opened his mouth to respond, but he shut it just as quickly.

"Mr. Dylan, there's a strange woman in here." Alice stood in the open archway that led into the living room and peered at me over her shoulder.

"Maybe she's his girlfriend," Nikki mock-whispered.

I pinched my eyes closed. Leave it to kids to find the most inopportune times to make comments.

Now Logan was the one smirking at me. "Are we interrupting?"

"No." I shook my head, irritation bubbling up inside me.

Logan chuckled. "Really? 'Cause you don't look so sure."

It was on the tip of my tongue to tell him there was nothing going on between Hattie and me. Only I couldn't seem to force the words past my lips.

Chapter Twenty

HATTIE

THERE WERE two little girls standing in Dylan's living room, not so quietly commenting on my presence. One thought I might be Dylan's girlfriend, and I didn't correct her. After all, that was what he wanted people to think, right?

I didn't know what to think. My head was spinning, and I was still reeling from the kiss Dylan and I had shared.

It was only a kiss, for Christ's sake. Get it together, Hattie. So what if it was a knock-your-socks-off and soak-your-panties kind of kiss? That didn't mean anything would come from it.

"What are your names?" I asked the two little girls.

"I'm Alice," the one with the pink headband said.

"And I'm Nikki." She looked over her shoulder, then zeroed in on me. "Are you Mr. Dylan's girlfriend?"

"No." Dylan's typically smooth voice came out gravelly. "She's just a friend."

My heart twisted painfully, but I kept my expression neutral. The kiss we'd shared was anything but friendly, but I could understand if he didn't want to get into it with a set of twins who couldn't be much older than five or six.

"These are Logan's daughters," he said, resting a hand on each of their heads. "His babysitter canceled, and the chief called him in, so they're going to hang out with us until their mom can come pick them up."

"Sounds fun." Thankfully, now that the storm had stopped, I could relax.

"Do you want to play go fish?" Nikki asked.

I gave her a soft smile. "Yeah, sure."

The girls took spots on the other side of the coffee table, then, in unison, glanced over at Dylan, who was still standing at the edge of the living room.

"Are you playing too?" Alice tilted her head.

With a sigh, he looked at the cushion beside me, his face screwed up as if he were afraid the couch would swallow him whole if he sat down. Reluctantly he made his way over and dropped down next to me, although through the whole exchange, he wouldn't look at me. Was I reading too much into it?

After a few rounds of go fish, my mood had lifted, and the anxiety that had overtaken me during the storm had disappeared.

Based on the smile Dylan wore, he was having fun too.

I loved hanging out with my nieces and nephews, and lately, I found myself preferring them over my siblings.

Maybe it was their lack of expectations or their ability to find the good in almost everything. Although settling down and having a few of my own was what I wanted, I was starting to wonder if it was in the cards for me.

If it wasn't, then I'd learn to be okay with being cool Aunt Hattie, I guessed.

"Do you girls like popcorn?" I held out the bowl Dylan and I had been munching from.

"Of course." They chirped at the same time, each sticking a hand into the bowl.

As I pulled it back, my arm brushed against Dylan's hand, and I could have sworn he flinched.

Seriously?

I stole a glance at him. Sure enough, as I watched him in my periphery, he scooted away subtly. He refused to meet my gaze, and now I was sure I wasn't reading too much into it. Since we'd kissed, he'd been acting strange.

I sighed. Of course the first guy in forever that I felt a connection with wasn't interested. That had happened to me more than a couple of times over the years, so I should be used to it.

Even so, it stung.

I could take a little solace, though, knowing that Dylan's strong moral code likely kept him from feeling as though he could be involved with one of his friend's sisters. As much as I wanted to, I couldn't blame him for that.

We played another round of go fish before the girls pulled out coloring books and crayons. I lay on the floor next to Nikki and helped her color a picture of Ariel. We were almost finished when the doorbell rang and the girls' mom came in.

"Why does Logan have to be so difficult about hiring a sitter who doesn't have one foot in the grave?" The woman huffed, frowning at Dylan. "I mean, I know why, but he's not his father. Just wish he would understand that."

Dylan shrugged. "I don't get it either, but you two know I'm happy to do it anytime you need."

As I stood, she caught sight of me and smiled.

"Hi, I'm Maggie." She stepped forward and stuck her hand out.

I shook it, studying her, knowing I recognized her. It only took a moment for my brain to catch up. "You're the pediatric surgeon at the hospital."

She nodded.

"My friend Cece talks about you all the time."

"Aw," she cooed. "Cece is such a sweetheart. I love her. I tried to poach her from the ER, but she wasn't having it. She loves it down there."

After chatting about Cece and how I'd gotten to know her over the last year, Maggie smiled and turned to Dylan.

"I like this one. She gets my approval."

His brows pulled together slightly. "What?"

"You two." She pointed between us. "You're dating, aren't you...?" A blush rose on her cheeks. "Sorry, I should know better than to listen to the gossip train."

Apprehension swirled in my belly. Why was the town even gossiping about me? I was never the talk of the town, and I preferred it that way. "I don't understand why they even care who I'm dating."

She smirked. "Oh honey, it's not you they care about. It's Half Moon Lake's most eligible bachelor." She nodded to Dylan.

Groaning, he narrowed his eyes on Maggie.

She held her hands up. "Sorry, don't shoot the messenger." With a chuckle, she surveyed the girls, who were still lying on the floor with their coloring books. "Time to go, girls."

Once she'd coaxed them out of here, I took the popcorn bowl and my empty soda bottle to the kitchen. After discarding the bottle and washing the bowl, I turned to find Dylan standing in the archway. He padded into the room, then, with a sigh, he leaned against the counter, crossing one ankle over the other.

My heart thumped in my ears the whole time, and the air was heavy with awkwardness.

Determined not to let discomfort settle between us, I dried my hands on the dishtowel and hung it up. Then I cleared my throat. "Can we talk about what happened earlier?"

Obviously, we had chemistry, but if what he felt for me wasn't strong enough to break bro-code or whatever, then I needed him to tell me that. It wasn't like I'd thrown myself at him, and from what I could tell, he was just as into it as I was. But at this point, I needed to know where we stood.

"Yeah. I'm sorry for walking away. I just needed a minute to gather my thoughts. I should have told you that."

That made sense. Frankly, the kiss had sent me spinning too, but why was he acting so weird now? I nodded. "Right. So—"

My words were cut off by the ringing of his cell phone. "Sorry," he said, digging it out of his pocket. "It's Aiden. Need to take this real quick." With that, he turned and strode to the sunroom. He answered as he stepped down into the room, and as he spoke to Aiden, he paced, using his free hand to gesture emphatically.

A yawn caught me by surprise as I strained to catch his mumbled words without any luck. I had to be up for work early tomorrow since I needed to submit payroll. We could talk tomorrow morning on our drive in. I grabbed my phone from the coffee table and shot Dylan a text to let him know I was headed to bed.

Once I lay down, though, I couldn't get comfortable. I tossed and turned, unable to shut off my brain. The kiss Dylan and I shared played over and over in my mind, and each time, I scolded myself for thinking about it. I'd spent the last two years, maybe longer, looking for a man I not only enjoyed spending time with but who ignited that blazing passion that Ashley and my friends had found. With just one kiss, Dylan had made me feel that.

If I were home, I would pull out my favorite toy and get myself off, then roll over and go to sleep. Here, I didn't have access to said toy. Plus, it was Dylan's lips on me, his fingers exploring, his cock deep inside me, that I really wanted.

I groaned in frustration, and then, with my bottom lip pulled between my teeth, I slid my hand under the blankets. Maybe I couldn't have exactly what I wanted, but that didn't have to stop me from taking advantage of being aroused for the first time in months.

Eyes closed, I imagined Dylan shirtless that night in my apartment. I slipped my fingers under the waistband of my panties, my core throbbing, and applied pressure to my clit, moving back and forth. I pictured Dylan storming into the room and slapping my hand away, then replacing it with his mouth.

My back arched off the bed, and I pulled my knees up, letting them fall open.

An image of him slipping a finger inside me as he continued to use his tongue floated through my mind. Moaning, I moved my hand faster, pumping two fingers in and out and rubbing my thumb in circles around my clit.

I trailed my other hand up under my shirt and pinched one nipple.

As I continued to pleasure myself, I pictured him crawling up my body, his cock long and thick as it entered me. When spasms overtook me, I turned my face into my pillow to muffle my moans.

It was all too much, but also not enough as I succumbed to the orgasm that enveloped me.

DYLAN

WHAT THE HELL was wrong with me? I couldn't really blame her for heading to bed and avoiding the guaranteed-to-be-awkward conversation we needed to have.

Huffing out a breath, I strode down the hall. As I passed her room, a noise, almost like a whimper, came from the other side, stopping me in my tracks. Shit. Maybe she was having another nightmare. I took a step back and inched over to her door to listen. The bed creaked and a faint moan hit my ears. It didn't sound like a distressed moan, but rather one filled with pleasure.

A zap of electricity shot straight down my spine. Was she touching herself?

Jesus Christ. I groaned as I braced against the doorframe and lowered my head. I was an asshole of epic proportions because a big part of me wanted to push through the door and demand she let me pleasure her.

I stepped back on the hardwood floor, ready to turn and get the hell out of here. But as I did, the boards creaked loudly under me.

Flinching at the sound, I held my breath. Awesome. I turned and started toward my bedroom before I did something insanely stupid. But when her door swung open, I froze again.

"Were you just standing outside my door?" she asked, barely more than a silhouette in the dark doorway. "Is everything okay?"

Swallowing thickly, I spun back toward her. The moment I did, though, I wished I hadn't. Her nipples poked through her thin tank top, and she was wearing nothing but panties with it. Now I regretted ever complaining about her sleep shorts. Because damn, my brain was currently short-circuiting.

She cleared her throat, garnering my attention. Blinking, I forced my head up and met her gaze.

"Um, yeah." What the hell did she want me to say? *I was listening to you getting yourself off, and it made me want to break the fucking door down*? No fucking way. I shifted my weight and glanced away. "You know...thought I heard something."

Her eyes widened, and a small gasp escaped her. Arms wrapped around her torso, she frowned. "And what did you think you heard?"

I arched a brow. Did she want me to spell it out? Confirm what she thought I heard. Hell no. I didn't need to replay the images that had run through my brain. Not until I was alone, at least.

"It doesn't matter." I kept my gaze on her face, determined not to let myself look anywhere else. But I lost that fight five seconds later and stole a quick glance down. Were her panties still damp from her arousal?

I adjusted myself and looked away.

Jesus, why was this so hard?

"I'm a bit confused."

My chest tightened, and I forced my attention back to her face. "Confused?"

"Yeah. You kissed me, then spent the rest of the evening acting weird. Now you look like you want to throw me onto the bed and have your way with me." She sighed. "If we both want the same thing, why are we fighting it?"

Shit, I really was an asshole. However, it didn't change things.

"It doesn't matter what I want when I can't have it." I folded my arms across my chest.

Her brows pulled together. "Why can't you have it?"

I bit back a groan. Did she really not understand? "Because you're Rhett's sister, not to mention I'm supposed to be protecting you."

"Right." With a sharp nod, she looked away.

"There are rules when it comes to these things."

"I get it." She sighed, her body deflating. "Rules shouldn't be broken unless it's important."

Frustration coursed through me, and I locked my jaw to keep from saying *bullshit*. Yeah, maybe she understood, but she also thought she wasn't important enough. And worse, she thought I felt the same way. But it was more complicated than that. If I screwed up, I'd not only put my friendship with Rhett and my job on the line, but her life as well. And that was the one thing I wouldn't gamble with.

"Good night Dylan." She turned, and then she was gone.

Fuck me.

Chapter Twenty-One

DYLAN

I FLICKED my wrist and checked my watch. Hattie would be down any minute. I'd gotten up even earlier than usual and put on a pot of coffee. Now I was making eggs and bacon. Hattie wouldn't eat the eggs, but even though she didn't eat breakfast, she loved bacon. Who didn't?

I only indulged on occasion, but since I'd discovered she liked it, I'd been making it regularly.

Anxiety gnawed at me as I turned off the stove. Would today be awkward? I hoped it wouldn't be.

After I'd gone to bed last night, I couldn't stop thinking about her. Her flushed cheeks and the mask of indifference she'd slid into place when she said she understood my reasons for not wanting to get involved were hell to deal with. Even worse? Thoughts of her touching herself kept popping into my head.

At the sound of her footsteps on the hardwood, I glanced over my shoulder.

"Good morning," she said with a smile that didn't quite reach her eyes.

Although she was dressed, her hair was still wet, and she hadn't done her makeup. She would grab a couple of strips of bacon and a cup of coffee, then she'd head back to finish getting ready. It was routine by now. What was abnormal today? She was missing that morning pep I'd started looking forward to.

"Good morning." I wasn't sure what to say to make this right, to explain to her that she was important. That, in fact, she was so important that I was afraid to cross a line we couldn't come back from.

If it were only the Rhett issue, I could argue that Jackson had already barreled over the line drawn between a guy and his best friend's sister. He'd gone as far as to marry her. Was that what I wanted? I couldn't say yes for sure, but then again, how would I know if I didn't give myself a chance to find out?

Regardless, the bigger issue was that it was stupid to get involved with a person I had been tasked with protecting. It complicated things and added a distraction I did not need. And after what Aiden told me last night, I needed to be even more focused. This guy wasn't letting up, and his moves were getting more daring.

"Coffee's in the pot." I tipped my head toward the coffee maker sitting on top of the granite countertop a foot away. "And your bacon is on the island."

"Oh." Her gaze bounced from the island to me before landing on the coffee pot. "Thank you."

She brushed past me, bringing with her the smell of fresh rain. When she opened the cabinet above the coffee pot and pulled out a mug, I found myself leaning closer to breathe her in.

Turning over her shoulder, she locked eyes with me. I couldn't help but drink her in. High cheekbones, face free of makeup, long lashes.

Christ, she was beautiful.

When her gaze locked on my lips, I blinked and turned away, forcing myself to focus on the eggs that needed to be plated.

The moment she left the kitchen, her absence was a physical ache.

Half an hour later, though, when her long locks brushed my forearm as she leaned over the middle console to place her backpack purse behind the seat, I was cursing her presence.

The drive to The Dock was awkward. She didn't speak and made sure to remain engrossed in her phone the whole time. It was equal parts torture as well. I hated the rift that had developed between us. And deep down, I knew there wasn't anything I could do to fix it.

Did I want her? Of course. Increasingly more so each moment I spent with her. But I didn't see how we could get what we wanted without comprising my friendship with Rhett, my job, and, most importantly, her safety.

Once I pulled up outside the restaurant, she threw the door open and thanked me without looking back.

I breathed a sigh of relief as I drove to the station, thankful for a few minutes of peace to get my shit together and stop obsessing about what stood between us.

Once I stepped inside the office, I headed straight to my desk, ready to focus on the case.

Aiden was already in front of his computer. "I have the footage pulled up from last night."

"Just mine?" I'd sent him my recordings before heading upstairs to bed and then inadvertently listened to Hattie pleasure herself.

I stiffened and blinked. *Do not think about that.*

Aiden cocked his head and narrowed his eyes, but after a moment, he said, "The neighbor sent me hers this morning."

"Perfect."

When Aiden called last night and told me that the woman who lived a few houses down had called about a possible intruder lurking in her backyard, I immediately downloaded the recordings from my exterior cameras.

"I went through mine briefly last night before sending them, but I'll go through them again while you watch the neighbors."

He nodded.

"I'm assuming none of the patrols found anything last night?"

He raised an eyebrow. "I would've updated you if they did."

"Yeah, of course." I shook my head.

"You okay?" He gave me a worried frown.

"Yup." I scoffed. "This guy is starting to get under my skin."

A chuckle rumbled out of him. "It could be unrelated, you know."

He'd said the same thing last night, but I highly doubted it.

"My gut tells me it isn't."

I sat at my computer and got to work watching the footage from my backyard. From there, I went through what the camera mounted above my garage had caught. But nothing stood out as odd.

All thoughts of Hattie had been pushed to the back of my

mind, but that changed when, on the screen, my SUV pulled into my driveway. I slowed the recording down and watched. Her car had been parked in my garage for the last week, and I had been parking outside.

Hattie stepped out of the vehicle, her long hair floating in the breeze, and as I came around the front of the car, she smiled at me. My stomach sank when I watched myself place a hand at the small of her back and usher her up the walkway.

Jesus, the look on her face when she glanced at me over her shoulder was like a punch to the gut. I was officially an asshole. Despite my attraction, I shouldn't have been touching her like that. But the more time I spent around her, the more I found myself looking for any reason to make contact with her. I wanted to touch her in the most intimate of ways, to feel her writhe under me as I brushed my fingers over her bare skin. Grip her thighs as I plowed into her—

"Dude," Aiden snapped, pulling me out of my thoughts.

Sucking in a harsh breath, I turned to him. What the fuck was his problem?

"What's up with you?" he asked, narrowing his eyes.

"What do you mean?"

Huffing, he rounded my desk and squinted at my computer screen. "Huh. Figures."

"What?" I shrugged. "I'm watching my footage."

"More like watching your girl."

A flash of irritation mixed with guilt spiked in my veins. "She's not my girl."

"Yeah, not buying it." He crossed his arms and loomed over me. "I've never known you to zone out like that." He pointed at his desk. "I had to say your name three times to get your attention."

I shook my head. Dammit. He was right about that. I hadn't realized he was speaking until he snapped at me.

"I'm just laser focused right now. I want to catch this guy."

I locked my jaw because part of me wanted to add *so I can figure things out with Hattie*. Because once we caught the stalker, the only obstacle we'd have to overcome would be Rhett. And I was hopeful that issue could be solved with a simple conversation. Rhett wouldn't love it if I dated Hattie, but he'd get over it. Eventually.

"You need to figure this shit out." Aiden pointed to the paused image of Hattie and me walking up the sidewalk. "Because this is one hell of a distraction for you, and I don't like it."

"Noted." I pushed away from my desk with a huff and stood. "Going to make a cup of coffee."

Was he right? Was I distracted?

And to think this was what I had been trying to avoid.

Fuck. I had no idea how to keep my mind from drifting to her. Even when she wasn't around, my thoughts were always about her.

Regardless, sleeping with her was a bad idea. Right?

Chapter Twenty-Two

HATTIE

Sighing, I snagged my bag off my chair, ready to head out to the front of the restaurant. Dylan had texted ten minutes ago to say he was on his way.

I strode out the door of my office and almost ran right into Ashley.

"Hey, you okay?"

Shoulders slumped, I took a deep breath. "Yeah, why?"

"You just seem…" She shrugged. "Not yourself."

"Just tired." I glanced away. "Ready for this whole stalker situation to be over."

Her intentions were good, but I didn't have the bandwidth for this conversation. And frankly, I had no clue how to explain the way I was feeling. Sad wasn't right. I understood where Dylan was coming from. He didn't feel as though he could put his friendship with my brother and his job on the line because we were attracted to each other, and I wouldn't ask him to.

Although after the last week and the kiss we shared last night, a part of me hoped that he saw the connection between us as more than just physical attraction.

That was the realization I'd finally come to last night after he kissed me. For the first time in years, I felt like someone was totally tuned into me. Focused on me, truly hearing me. Like my brothers were with their wives, like Jackson was with Ashley. Even how my dad was with Mom. He was quiet about it, sure, but it didn't go unnoticed. Ultimately that was what I wanted. Someone who got me a Cherry Coke out of the fridge or pulled me into a hug before I even had to voice that I was upset.

Except Dylan didn't feel the same way.

Ashley narrowed her eyes at me, and I moved to brush past her. Thankfully she stepped to the side and didn't push the conversation, but two steps past her, she spoke again.

"Hattie."

I looked back at her over my shoulder.

"You know if you need to talk, I'm here."

I nodded. My family drove me nuts sometimes, but I knew every one of them would be there if I needed them.

The minute I hit the dining room, I could make out Dylan's deep voice, and a shiver ran down my spine. Breath held, I sought him out. When I found him, he was propped up on the end of the bar, talking with Michael, Paul, and Josh. I drank him in. He was still wearing a suit, but he'd removed the jacket. His badge hung around his neck, and his weapon was clipped to his belt.

As I came closer, he turned his head, his dark eyes piercing me with intensity. There was no stopping the butterflies that took flight in my belly.

Jesus, Hattie. At least try to get a grip.

I swallowed, unsure of how to even act in his presence, as I stopped a foot from him. Because the way he looked at me? It sent a thrill through me while simultaneously putting me on edge.

With a chuckle, Michael looked back and forth between us. "Trouble in paradise?"

Dylan wrapped his arm around my shoulders and pulled me into his side. "Nah, man. It's great." Tipping his head, he pressed his lips to my temple.

Without any thought, I melted into him and sighed. This was what I'd needed all day.

But I didn't understand what was going on. This couldn't be one-sided. He had to feel this connection between us.

We stayed like that, with his arm wrapped around me, while he talked with the bar regulars. As the minutes ticked on, hope bloomed in my chest. And each time he smoothed his hand up and down my arm, a myriad of sensations coursed through me.

Maybe he'd come to the same realization I had. Maybe he did want to pursue this.

But by the time we were in the car and driving away from The Dock, the hope I'd been feeling had completely disappeared.

A switch had been flipped, and now he seemed pissed. Had it been a rough day? Or was he upset with me? For the life of me, I couldn't understand what I had done in the last ten minutes to cause his mood to shift.

"How was work?" I asked, hands clasped in my lap.

"Fine," he clipped. He was rigid, his body ramrod straight, with a death grip on the steering wheel and a tic in his jaw. Definitely pissed.

Chest aching, I turned and looked out the window.

When "Just a Kiss" by Lady A started playing on the radio, I reached to turn it off. I'd heard it earlier while I was streaming music from my phone, and it had instantly reminded me of Dylan. As I went for the knob, Dylan did too. Our fingers brushed, and he yanked his hand back like my touch had burned him.

My stomach bottomed out as I sat back in my chair, blinking away tears. I was being ridiculous.

I hated this for both of us. Obviously, he was uncomfortable with my presence after the kiss, and I didn't want him to feel like he had no choice because he'd made a promise to my over-stepping brother.

But I couldn't go back to my apartment alone. Not with the stalker still out there. Maybe staying with one of my siblings or my parents would be better.

We drove the rest of the way in silence, and once we were in the house, I spun to him.

"Maybe I should go stay with my parents."

"What?" His eyes widened, and he took a step back. "Why would you do that?"

I shrugged. "It might be better."

"No, it wouldn't be." He crossed his arms in front of his chest. "They can't protect you. Not like I can."

I sighed, my chest deflating. "It has to be better than dealing with this awkward tension."

His expression darkened, but he didn't respond.

"Look, I know it's my fault." I fiddled with my earring. I didn't want to fight with him. I just wanted him to understand. "I misread signals, and I've made things awkward."

He groaned. "Hattie, you didn't misread anything."

"Yes I did. It's fine. I get it. But…" I squared my shoulders, determined to get through to him. I'd give him an out. Let him know that he didn't need to keep his promise to Rhett. I would take the blame if my brother got upset. "This situation isn't fair to either of us. I know you want to keep your promise to Rhett, but now I've made it complicated. So I think the best solution is for me to go stay with my parents. I'll call my brother too. Let him know it was my choice."

Why did he look even more pissed off than he had a minute ago?

DYLAN

A solution, my ass. Did she not understand that I was her best chance in this situation? Like hell would I let her stay anywhere without me, and it had nothing to do with my promise to Rhett.

Her expression was desperate, pleading, but I wasn't sure whether she wanted me to agree or disagree.

"I think it'll be for the best…"

The best for whom, exactly?

"It'll make everything easier."

Was that what I wanted? Easy? A solution? When the

woman I wanted was staring at me, begging me to say something?

Fuck it.

Either way, I was screwed. That was obvious after today.

"Hattie." I closed the distance and cupped her face with both hands. "Need you to hear me right now. You did not misread anything."

Her eyes popped open wide, and her lips parted. "I didn't?"

I zeroed in on her mouth, ready to lean in and get another taste of everything I'd been thinking about all day. But first I needed her to understand.

"No." I smirked. "I want you so badly I spent the whole day thinking about it. I've been so distracted thinking about you, about kissing you again."

"Really? I—" She snapped her mouth shut and blinked several times. "What...I mean..." She huffed, her breath warm on my neck as she peered up at me. "I don't understand."

Chuckling, I caressed her cheeks with my thumbs. "I know, and that's my fault. So I'll make sure I'm really clear. I want you, Hattie." I moved one hand down to cup the side of her neck and brushed my thumb along her lower lip. "I can't think about anything but you. I thought that if I kept my distance, I could stay focused, because I would never forgive myself if something happened to you. But after today, it's clear that regardless of what happens between us, I'll be distracted. You're all I think about."

The corners of her mouth lifted into a smile. "And my brother?"

Shrugging, I grasped her waist and pulled her closer. "I'm not going to lie to him. He might be pissed when he finds out, but he'll get over it."

I brought her flush against my body, and she gripped my shoulders, her breath hitching. When her gaze locked on my lips, I tilted forward and paused an inch away, letting her take the lead.

I was done fighting this, but if she had any doubts, I'd back off and give her time.

Chapter Twenty-Three

HATTIE

I SLID my hands around to the back of his head. God, I wanted him more than I'd ever wanted anything before. No way was I going to muddle it up by asking him to define what we were doing.

Popping up on my toes, I pressed my mouth to his. The instant our lips were fused together, he backed me up against the railing of the staircase, devouring and exploring every inch of my mouth with his tongue.

He ran his hands over my hips and down my thighs,

pausing on the bare skin just past the hem of my skirt. He lingered there for what felt like a lifetime before slowly trailing his fingers under my skirt, lighting up my nerve endings as he went. Gripping my ass tightly, he lifted me.

I wrapped my legs around his waist and let my head fall back as he kissed a path along my jaw and nipped at my ear.

"Dylan, please." I moaned as I rotated my hips, rubbing against him.

"Please, what?" he asked, moving down my neck, pulling my blue sweater farther off my shoulder and pressing wet kisses over my collarbone.

"I need you," I panted. "So desperately I feel like I'm going to explode."

He pulled back and rested his forehead against mine. "Me too, baby. Me too."

My stomach fluttered as his words permeated through the haze of desire that had overtaken me.

"I can't wait to taste you on my tongue." Clutching me to him, he headed up the stairs.

I clung to him tightly, sucking on his neck.

Groaning, he dug his fingers into the flesh of my ass. "I want to know how you sound when you're screaming my name."

With a chuckle, I pulled back to look at him. "Cocky, are we?"

"Did you think about me last night?" He raised one brow.

Heat crept up my neck and into my face as he turned the corner at the top of the steps and strode into his bedroom. He tossed me onto his bed and loomed over me, studying me with an intensity that made me squirm. Was I brave enough to tell him that yes, I'd imagined he was the one bringing me pleasure?

I tracked his movements as he slid a hand to the holster at his side, unclipped it from his belt and turned toward the nightstand. After he pressed a series of buttons on top of what looked like a digital alarm clock, a drawer popped out. He placed his weapon inside and closed it before turning his focus back on me.

"Please, tell me. Did you imagine it was me touching you?" He pulled the lanyard his badge hung from over his head and tossed it on the nightstand. "Because it's all I've thought about."

Propping myself up on my elbows, I pulled my bottom lip into my mouth and nodded. He made me feel seen and safe, like I could say or do anything, and he would get it.

"Show me." He tipped his head in my direction and loosened the tie at his throat.

"What?" My core throbbed as I thought about him watching me pleasure myself. Why did that idea turn me on so much?

He slid the silky material from around his neck, and an image of him using it to bind my hands flashed through my mind. Ever since he'd mentioned handcuffing me to my bed, I couldn't stop fantasizing about it. As the idea popped into the forefront of my mind, I couldn't stop myself from looking down at where his handcuffs were attached to his belt.

"That's right. I forgot you like the thought of being cuffed to my bed. Being at my mercy." He pulled them out and threw them next to me on the mattress, then went back to slowly undressing, undoing the top buttons of his shirt.

My skin buzzed with anticipation. I never thought I'd like that. But with him, in this moment, I desperately wanted it.

He popped the button at one cuff, and then the other. "But first, bend your knees. Let me see you."

Heat flooded me as he licked his lips when his gaze zeroed in on the spot between my legs. God, I was thankful I'd worn my favorite lacy purple thong today.

As arousal coursed through me, I smirked. "Kinda liking bossy Dylan right now."

"Good," he said, undoing one button at a time. "Now show me how you touched yourself when you were thinking about me." He worked his shirt out of the waistband of his pants and undid the last button.

I took in the defined lines of muscles that ran along his chest and abs. My left arm trembled as I kept myself propped up and slid my right hand between my legs and rubbed myself through the lacy material.

He shook his head and smirked. "Get rid of those."

My skin flushed hotter. I'd never had an experience like this. Though I had no clue what I was doing, I wasn't about to let it stop.

Arching my back, I lifted my ass off the mattress and slid the thong down my legs.

"Now the rest of it," he gritted out.

His pupils blew out, watching me as I removed the rest of my clothing.

"That's a good girl." In rough motions, he pushed his shirt off his shoulders, then he let it fall to the floor.

His words gave me confidence to bring my knees back up and hold his heated stare while my fingers drifted between my legs. Hesitantly, I ran them down my slit and then back up to circle my clit.

Oh, god. That felt good, but it wasn't enough.

"Open your legs wider, Hattie," he rasped out. "I want to see all of you."

Obediently, I pulled my knees apart, letting them fall to the sides. "I want *you*."

"Me too." He smirked, bringing his hands to his belt and unfastening it. "I can't wait to feel you gripping my cock. But first I want you to show me what you like." With one quick movement, he yanked his belt from around his waist and dropped it next to the cuffs.

My mouth fell open. Was he going to spank me with that? My core tightened at the idea.

Jesus. What was it about this man that made me want to do a whole host of dirty things with him?

He popped the button of his pants and removed them along with his boxers. Then he stood to his full height again. "More, Hattie. I want you to touch yourself like you did last night."

Bottom lip caught between my teeth, I took in his perfectly toned body, pausing to admire his thick shaft. The need to fall to my knees in front of him and wrap my lips around the tip sped up my movements, and I rubbed my clit faster. The way all his attention was focused on me, drinking me in, only added to the pleasure I was giving myself.

Without looking away, he pulled a condom from the nightstand drawer. Then he fisted his cock and rolled it down his hard length. Pressure built quickly in my core as I continued to move my fingers against my sensitive skin, watching his every move.

Finally, he got on his knees between my legs, using his hands on my inner thighs to push my legs even farther apart. His gaze never strayed from the junction of my thighs.

"Fuck, baby. I could watch you touch yourself all day. So hot."

"I'm so close," I moaned.

He slapped my hand away and grabbed his belt. A whimper slipped through my lips as my arousal skyrocketed.

"Did you want me to use this?"

"To spank me?" Oh my god. Was I really going to let him do that?

A seductive chuckle slipped past his lips. "You're a dirty girl, aren't you?"

"Only with you." The words were laced with so much truth.

"I'll use the belt to bind your hands. It won't leave marks on your perfect skin like the cuffs would. But only if you want that."

I swallowed down any remaining nerves, because *fuck, yes, I did*, and nodded.

"Need your words, Hattie."

"Yes, I want you to."

His smirk went straight to my core. "Lift your arms above your head and bring your wrists together." He looped the belt into a figure eight and hovered over me.

I did as he asked, and as he slipped the band of leather over one hand, then the other, the rough leather scraped deliciously against my skin. He lifted my hands off the bed slightly and tightened the restraint.

His lips brushed against mine and he pulled back, searching my face. "You okay?"

"Yeah."

"If at any point you're not, you need to tell me. Okay?"

I nodded. The sincerity etched in his features settled deep inside me. He wasn't just giving me what I wanted. He was making sure I was comfortable too.

He raised an eyebrow, silently reminding me that he needed my words.

"Yeah, I'm good."

He grazed my arm with his fingertips, causing goose bumps to erupt in his wake, and stopped at my breast, running his thumb back and forth over my nipple until I was writhing. And when his hand slipped lower and he found my clit, I was sure I'd never experienced anything like this.

"I need—" I panted, suddenly unable to form a coherent thought.

"What do you need?"

"You. Need you." I'd never needed someone as much as I

needed him in this moment. I'd imagined this. Hoped for it. But it far surpassed my expectations.

"Where?" His sheathed length pressed at my entrance. "Here?"

"Yes." My arms lifted involuntarily, but the tension around my wrists reminded me I couldn't pull them apart, leading me to relax once again.

Teasing me, he slid his thick head along my seam. "What about tomorrow?"

"Tomorrow?" I asked breathlessly.

"Yes. Will you need me tomorrow too?"

I nodded as I met his heated gaze.

"And next month?" He inched forward slowly, spreading me, forcing my walls to adjust to his size.

"Yes."

He shoved deep inside me, pulling a gasp from my lips. The immense feeling that overtook me from being connected to him was like nothing I'd ever felt before.

"You feel so damn perfect." He slowly pulled almost all the way out and then pushed back in again.

"More," I whimpered.

"Want you like this every day." He dragged his cock back out and plunged into me again.

No one had ever wanted me like that. With every thrust, I could feel his desperate need for me. I never wanted the sensation to end.

His movements picked up, and he thrust into me again and again. It was the perfect combination of rough and gentle. Over and over, he slammed into me, hitting that sensitive spot deep inside.

My walls tightened as I arched into him, meeting him stroke for stroke. Bracing on his elbows, he stared intently into my eyes, watching me as the pressure built in my core.

"Dylan." As the first waves of my climax hit me hard, there was no holding back a scream.

"That's it, baby." Two more hard thrusts. "Come for me."

And I did, my chest pressed into his and my hands clenched into fists.

He threw his head back with a groan, his cock pulsing inside me. He drove into me quickly, over and over, as we rode out our orgasms. Then he collapsed on top of me.

We lay there for a few moments. I didn't care that it was hard to breathe. Being joined with him like this was so worth it.

Finally, he pulled out and leaned back on his knees, a smirk appearing on his face. "As much as I like this view, I should probably free you."

I smiled, not minding the idea of being laid out for him like this at all.

Leaning forward, he undid the belt's buckle so I could shimmy one hand out of its enclosure before sliding the other one out.

"Next time I can restrain you to the headboard, if you want."

Next time. My body sagged into the mattress at his words.

He climbed off the bed and stood. "Give me a minute."

As he disappeared into the bathroom, I sat up, eyeing his dress shirt on the floor. By the time he stepped back into the room, I'd slipped into it and fastened two buttons.

When he sauntered out of the bathroom, his eyes flared. "Don't wear any panties under that tonight."

I raised an eyebrow. "And what if I don't listen?"

With two big steps, he closed the space between us, smirking. I kinda liked getting him fired up. He backed me against the wall, then ran his hands up my thighs and gripped my bare ass.

"Good girl," he rasped against my ear. "Now let's go downstairs and figure out dinner. Then I plan to have you for dessert."

Chapter Twenty-Four

HATTIE

AFTER FINALLY CONVINCING Tyler to go home, that we were fine, Dylan locked the front door of The Dock. A few weeks ago, Rhett had asked me if I could close up the restaurant for him. At that time, I obviously hadn't realized that I would have a stalker, so I'd agreed.

Dylan turned and stalked across the dining room toward me, his intent clear in his heated gaze.

My stomach flipped, and the closer he got, the louder my pulse pounded in my ears.

Since Monday, when things had finally changed between us, I'd found myself the focus of that intense look every time we were together. While we made dinner on Monday night and waking up in his arms yesterday morning. Even when he stopped by yesterday to pick up lunch.

Although we hadn't really talked about what we were doing, he'd said he wouldn't lie to Rhett. But did that mean he wanted a relationship with me? I doubted he was keen on telling his best friend that he was casually hooking up with his sister, so I assumed he wanted a more long-term situation.

I sure did. Though I didn't need a label, I was eager to find out exactly where this was going. It had only been two days, though, so my stupid insecurities needed to quiet down.

The stalker hadn't texted since I'd blocked the new number, so it was hard not to hope that he'd moved on. Dylan was beyond frustrated that they still had no leads or breaks in the case, and I couldn't blame him. I wanted the whole thing to be over.

"I never thought I'd be happy to discover a place didn't have cameras," he said as he quickly closed the rest of the space between us. "Come here, baby." He grabbed my waist and pulled me closer.

Why did I smile like an idiot any time he used that term?

Probably because the affection in his tone each time he spoke that word, *baby*, made me feel special.

Jesus, I was already falling for this man, and it had been less than two weeks. Was that even possible?

With a smirk, I pressed a hand to his chest. "You promised you'd help unbox the wine that came in today, remember?"

"I promise I'll help you with the wine when I drop you off in the morning." He leaned forward, his lips close to my ear. "Right now, I'm desperate to feel your lips and then get you home so I can spend all night inside you."

My core throbbed with so much anticipation I had to squeeze my legs together to relieve some of the tension.

He trailed his lips along my jaw and claimed my mouth, coaxing me to open as he backed me up against the table. I gripped the back of his head, holding him to me as our tongues tangled with desperation.

Damn, I could curse myself for wearing pants today. There was too much material between us as I ground against his leg.

As if he could read my mind, he dug his fingers into my hips and pulled back.

"To your office."

I blinked. "My office?"

"If you want my mouth on your pussy, then go to your office and wait for me." Giving me a dark smile, he turned me that way and swatted my ass. "Preferably naked and spread across your desk."

The way he took charge and talked filthy to me sent a thrill through my body. It wasn't something I'd ever thought I'd need, but his confidence totally did it for me.

"What are you going to do?"

"Double-check the side and patio doors."

Nodding, I headed for my office. I hadn't made it more than two steps before a loud crash came from the patio seating area at the back of the restaurant. We both froze and turned that way.

Between the lights in the dining room and the darkened sky, I couldn't really see anything.

"Fuck, someone's out there." He grabbed my hand and pulled me toward the hallway that led to the offices.

"I didn't see anyone. Are you sure?" I slowed my feet, making him turn to me. "It was probably just the wind or an animal."

With a shake of his head, he turned and tugged me forward again. "No, I definitely saw someone." He pulled out his phone and swiped the screen before dropping the device back into his pocket. "Hey, you outside?"

I tilted my head, confused, until I noticed a small earbud in his ear.

Waving me into my office, he stood in the doorway, gaze focused down the hallway that led back out to the dining room. "Yeah, we're fine. But do me a favor. Check the back. Someone was looking in the window."

DYLAN

THE FIVE MINUTES before my phone rang felt like an eternity. Fuck, I hoped Ethan was calling to tell me he'd caught the guy. But if that were the case, it would have taken a whole lot longer. When Aiden had suggested putting a patrol car out front tonight, I'd argued at first. Once he'd mentioned yet another complaint he'd received regarding someone lurking around my neighborhood, I'd given in, though, agreeing that it was better to be safe. She was never the first person here or the last. Until tonight. A closing shift was a totally different ballgame, since it was almost eleven now.

I tapped my ear, answering Ethan's call. "Whatcha got?"

"No one's out here."

"I definitely saw someone."

"Sorry, sir. He must have gone into the water. Otherwise he would have had to come past me."

That was exactly what I figured too. The building backed up to the water, and since there was a fence separating the marina area from the restaurant, there really was only one way in and out from the back. Unless he jumped into the water to get around.

"He could have gone out in the water, I guess. Or maybe he disappeared into the woods on the far side before I got back there. But I didn't see anything disturbed or tracks leading to or from the back patio."

I locked my jaw. If he knocked over a chair, he could have had time to pick it up before fleeing. Regardless, I knew what I'd seen. Although I had been in a lust-induced haze. Could I have been so hyper focused on getting Hattie out of her clothes that I imagined someone watching us through the back window?

This was exactly why I'd wanted to avoid crossing the line with her. How could I remain focused on the investigation when all I thought about was touching her, tasting her, feeling her grip my dick?

The answer to my question was obvious. I couldn't do my best to find her stalker while thoughts of her constantly plagued me. Maybe I should've let her go stay with her parents until we'd caught this guy.

"Sir, you there?"

"Yeah. We're heading out now. Meet me at the front door." I hung up and turned to look at Hattie. Her cheeks were flushed, and she was wearing a soft but worried smile.

I wasn't sure how much longer I could keep doing this. I needed to focus on catching this guy. My gut was saying someone was out there, and there was no way I could let anything happen to her.

Chapter Twenty-Five

HATTIE

WHEN WE GOT HOME last night, Dylan insisted I sleep in his bed like I had the two nights prior, and though he joined me, he sat up against the headboard and focused on his phone, essentially shutting me out. It was awkward, to say the least. At the restaurant, he had been desperate for me, but once we were in bed, it was almost like he didn't even want me there.

Maybe I was reading too deeply into things. He'd sworn he saw someone out back, and I believed it, so maybe the issue was that he was frustrated with how the night had gone. And he did make a point to rub my shoulder and brush his hand along my thigh once or twice before I finally rolled over and went to sleep.

Yeah, I must have been reading into things that weren't there.

I stepped into the kitchen, and when I wasn't hit with the familiar scents of fresh-cooked bacon and coffee, I froze.

I was surveying the kitchen, confused about the change in routine, when a hand landed on my shoulder. Startling, I whipped around, only to find Dylan standing close.

"Good morning." He hurried past me toward the kitchen table, where he grabbed his laptop bag and threw it over his shoulder.

"I'm heading into the station early today," he said. "Ethan's outside. He's going to drive you to work today."

"Okay..." I ran my hand up my arm and clutched my bicep. "I could get ready really quick and ride in with you."

He shook his head, attention averted. "No. It's fine. Ethan can take you."

I refused to be the whiny, clingy girlfriend, no matter how badly I wanted to scream out *no, I want you to take me.*

"I'll stop by to pick up lunch again today." He leaned forward and brushed his lips against my temple.

"Alright. See you later."

Without a backward glance, he strode to the front door and closed it firmly behind him.

What the hell? Had he changed his mind? After last night, had he realized that being with me wasn't worth the drama? If that were the case, I couldn't blame him. Even though I tried not to harp on that thought while I got ready for the day, I failed miserably. The first thing I encountered at work were the cases of wine that he'd promised to help with.

I sighed. He was busy. That was all. At least that's what I

tried to convince myself of for the millionth time. He was busy, and he didn't need a clingy, overbearing girlfriend.

I'd almost believed it until I pulled out my phone a few hours later and clicked on his text message.

Dylan: Hey, I can't make it over to grab lunch. Could you send someone over with it?

Weird. But again, he was busy.

Me: Sure, no problem.

Dylan: Thanks.

I would run it over. That way I could see him for a few minutes. Ethan had told me this morning that he would be around and that if I had to leave the building to text him, so I shot off a quick message and put together the order.

By the time I made it to the entrance of the restaurant, Ethan was already waiting for me. The drive over to the station only took ten minutes, but when I stepped up to the officer at the front desk and told him I was here with Dylan Gray's lunch order, I was starting to feel nervous about my decision.

What if he asked for the food to be delivered because he didn't want to see me? Or he was too busy and didn't have time? Would he be annoyed that I'd shown up?

I spun the beaded bracelet on my left wrist, willing my nerves to settle. I was being ridiculous.

A few moments later, the officer behind the counter returned and held out a hand, gesturing to the bag. "He says you can leave it here."

"Thanks." Masking my disappointment with a smile, I turned and hurried back out to Ethan, feeling stupid. I understood that his career was important and that he was busy, but was he really so overloaded with work that he couldn't take one minute to say hi?

After focusing on work and hearing nothing else from Dylan, I was more than ready to see him by the time five o'clock came around. We would have dinner together like usual, maybe watch some TV. Then we'd fall into bed together, and I could stop worrying that he'd changed his mind.

But when Ethan met me at the door at the end of the day, disappointment swamped me again.

"Where's Dylan?"

He shrugged. "Still at the station, I assume. You ready?"

Once I was buckled in the passenger seat of Ethan's patrol car, I shot off a text to Dylan.

> Me: Everything okay?

> Dylan: Yup

WITH A SIGH, I tried again.

> Me: Will you be home for dinner?

> Dylan. No.

> Me: You sure everything's okay?

> Dylan: Yup.

Now I was spiraling. I needed more than a one-word answer from him.

> Me: Want to tell me what's going on?

> Dylan: We can talk when I get home.

Well, that didn't sound great. If nothing was wrong, he

wouldn't want to talk. I swallowed the lump in my throat and turned toward the window.

By the time nine o'clock came and went without any word from Dylan, it was clear something had changed.

I wasn't sure why, but the message had been received. Loud and clear. I didn't need to wait up to hear whatever explanation he was going to give. It wouldn't matter.

Feeling sad and stupid, I went upstairs, took a shower, and climbed into my own bed. Maybe I'd pushed too hard on Monday, and he wasn't actually ready for a relationship.

I wouldn't make that mistake twice.

Chapter Twenty-Six

DYLAN

"You'll be here, then?" my dad verified for the third time since we'd been on the phone that I would, in fact, be making it home for my mom's birthday in three weeks.

"Yes, shouldn't be a problem." This case better be wrapped up by then. If not, I'd lose my fucking mind.

"Okay." Dad sighed. "Just want this party to be perfect for her."

My dad had been planning this for months, and given it was my mom's sixtieth, he wanted to go all out.

A smile lifted my lips at the idea of bringing Hattie home to meet my parents. "Mind if I bring someone with me?"

Was it too soon for this step? Maybe...

I glanced up at the opening to the kitchen in hopes of seeing her. She was usually down by eight thirty, yet the clock was inching toward eight forty.

"Oh," my dad started, his tone suddenly low. "Did you and Becca get back together?"

"No." My gut twisted at the thought. Why on earth would he think that? "Not Becca. I'm dating someone new."

"That's great." He perked up, his voice jovial again. "Definitely bring her."

We chatted about Hattie and plans for the party for a few minutes, but when a knock sounded at my front door, I said my goodbyes and hustled for the entryway.

After checking my doorbell camera, I opened the door to the dark-haired man cautiously.

Quickly, he introduced himself as Seabass. Everything about the guy screamed special ops, even his name. Had to be a nickname.

When, in his next breath, he explained that Kyle had called and told him I could use his help, I glared.

"Kyle did what?" I must have misheard the guy.

He cocked his head. "I'm gathering he didn't mention I was coming?"

No, Hattie's overbearing pain-in-the-ass brother did not mention he was sending a fucking frogman to assist me with my case.

Jesus. Red crowded my vision. I'd never noticed until this debacle began just how nosy and over-stepping Hattie's family could be.

"He did not."

On Sunday, Kyle had made it clear he was frustrated. So was I, but I assumed he had faith in me, in the entire damn police department. Clearly, I was wrong. Yesterday, Aiden and I had spent fifteen hours combing through footage from outside cameras around and near The Dock and examining the names of buyers we received from the place that had sold the blue lady orchids. So far, we were only looking at buyers who'd provided addresses located in North Carolina, but none lived here in Half Moon Lake.

I didn't need more help. I needed this douchebag to make a mistake. I needed him to show himself. But Seabass worked for the private security firm Kyle had considered working for before ultimately choosing to remain in Half Moon Lake with Tina and the kids. That meant the guy had come all the way from New York.

Not to mention it wasn't Seabass's fault Kyle hadn't bothered to mention to me that he'd asked his friend to come assist.

I waved him in and led him into the kitchen. I spent the next fifteen minutes updating him on where we were on the case.

Hattie stepped into the kitchen as the coffeepot was brewing.

"Coffee's almost ready, and this is Seabass. Your brother sent him to help us out."

"Oh, that works out perfectly." The smile she directed at me came off forced. She was probably even more annoyed than I was about Kyle over-stepping. "Now you don't have to ask Ethan to stay here with me today. Seabass can."

Damn. I'd forgotten that she was off today since she'd closed for Rhett on Wednesday night. The smile she wore when she greeted Seabass was anything but forced. Almost flirty.

What the fuck? I planned to come home to give her a case update after her text last night, so it was strange to find she was already asleep. On top of that, she was back in the guest room rather than in my bed. I was tempted to climb in beside her, but I didn't want to wake her. All this shit was stressful. She probably needed the rest. So after a kiss on the forehead, I went back to my bed.

Now she was flirting with this asshole? Was she pissed that I'd worked late last night? Becca had always taken issue with the unpredictable hours, so I shouldn't be surprised. Although I had hoped that Hattie would be different, and until this moment, she'd seemed to be.

But not only had I seen it in my own relationships, but in relationships throughout the station. I wanted this to work, though, so first, I had to get rid of Seabass. Then we could talk.

"I'm planning to work from home today," I blurted out.

Hattie narrowed her eyes at me. What the hell? Was she seriously upset about it? Seabass cocked a brow, clearly reading into the expression the same way. But I didn't care, and I sure as hell wasn't leaving her here with him all day.

"You should head to the station," I told Seabass. "Getting a fresh pair of eyes on what we have so far would be good. I'll let Aiden know you're coming."

Fifteen minutes later, Seabass was gone, and I was exhaling a sigh of relief. I'd lose my damn mind if I had to watch Hattie smile at and laugh with this guy any longer. Especially when she was giving me nothing but indifference.

I turned to head back into the kitchen and almost collided with her. She jumped back, then turned, as if trying to brush past me. With a sharp breath in, I grabbed her forearm, but when she flinched and pulled away, I immediately released her and stepped back.

What the hell was going on?

I was fucking great at my job, but unfortunately, I couldn't read minds. We needed to have a conversation. Becca and I hadn't communicated well, and I'd learned the importance of being transparent—and asking for transparency from my partner—a little too late in that relationship.

"What's up with you?" I crossed my arms in front of my chest, bracing myself, certain a blow was coming.

As much as it killed me to think that Hattie couldn't handle the way my job affected my personal life, I'd rather know now than weeks or months down the road when I was more invested. Even now, though, I was already pretty damn invested. It was why I was busting my ass to solve this fucking case. For her. For us.

"What do you mean?" Her words were laced with feigned nonchalance. Maybe the act would fool most people, but I'd been trained to read body language and expressions, as well as tone of voice. And there was no hiding her stiff posture or the pain swimming in her eyes.

I sighed and let my hands fall to my sides. Talking about it now would hopefully allow us to figure out the best way to handle issues we were met with in the future. I wasn't planning to let her walk away without putting up a fight.

"I thought it was weird that you fell asleep in the guest room last night, but brushed it off, assuming you were tired and didn't want me to wake you when I came in."

She tilted her head, her eyes narrowing, but she didn't respond.

"Then this morning, you were openly flirting with Seabass."

She opened her mouth and sucked in a breath like she was ready to argue, but I went on before she could.

"And just now, you literally flinched at my touch. Please, if you're mad at me, just tell me. Because I'm at a loss. What did I do to upset you?"

She stared at me for what felt like forever before she sighed and wrapped her arms tightly around her stomach. "I'm not mad. I realize that we haven't had a real conversation about what's going on between us. But I'm not interested in anything temporary..."

Good. Neither was I, but what did that have to do with her strange behavior?

"And I don't know...maybe you changed your mind," she rambled on. "But it's fine. I got your message yesterday."

My message? Changed my mind? About what? What the hell was she talking about? We barely spoke yesterday, other than for a minute before I left for work and a few random texts throughout the day. None of those messages were about anything important. Were they? Maybe I needed more sleep, because my brain was having a hard time putting the pieces together.

She shifted on her feet and looked away, her throat bobbing.

"Hattie, if you've decided you can't handle my job, I understand. I've heard it before. It's a lot."

She frowned, her brows pulled low as she studied me.

"I'm usually good at deciphering things, but I'll be honest, I'm lost."

She locked eyes with me, her irises swirling with indecision.

"Can we sit and talk?" I waved at the open archway that led into the living room.

With a nod, she shuffled to one sofa. Rather than sitting across from her, I sat right next to her so our thighs touched. Then I forced myself to give her a smirk. "Maybe my brain is too full of thoughts of you and this case, because it's not working too well. But I need you to spell it out for me. What's the problem?"

She sighed, head bowed and fingers fiddling with the hem of her shorts. "On Wednesday, after you thought you saw someone outside the restaurant, it seemed like you didn't want me in your bed. Then yesterday, you had Ethan drive me. That's fine, I swear. But then you didn't even come out to say hi when I brought your lunch to the station."

My stomach sank. *She* delivered my lunch? Shit. If I'd

known, I would have had Chris send her back. Not sure why he didn't say something. And why the fuck didn't Ethan give me a heads-up?

Hey asshole, probably because you haven't told any of them she's officially your girl.

As far as any of them knew, we were only letting people think that in order to draw out the stalker.

With a huff, Hattie went on, her words tumbling out quickly, making it difficult to keep up. "I texted you in the car when Ethan brought me back here, but you only responded with one-word answers and then you didn't text to let me know you'd be late. I waited up, but when I started dozing on the couch and you still weren't home, I went to bed." She looked down at her hands, wringing them. "It felt like maybe you had changed your mind. Or that you weren't looking to get involved in a relationship." She slowly looked back up, meeting my gaze once more before squaring her shoulders. "I need to know what we're doing. If I don't, then I'll end up listening to my stupid insecurities like I have been for the last twenty-four hours."

Gut twisting, I grasped her hand. "I'm sorry if I've been distant and not super fucking clear about my intentions." I pressed a kiss to her knuckles. "I have not changed my mind, and I sure as hell don't want something casual or temporary."

She smiled, and a blush crept up her neck. "Really?"

"Yeah." I chuckled. "You're the reason I've been hyper focused on finding this guy since Wednesday night. The thought of him watching us, getting that close to you that night, made me angry and scared all at the same time. If anything happened to you because I was distracted, I'd never forgive myself."

She squeezed my hand. "Nothing's going to happen to me."

With my hands on her hips, I guided her onto my lap. She

melted into my chest and let me hold her. Let me breathe in the intoxicating smell of rain. My dick jumped in my pants, but right now, that was not the priority. Making sure Hattie knew exactly what I wanted was. I was not walking away from her until she understood that I wanted her, insecurities and all. I couldn't fault her for them. Not when I had my own. And the only way this would work was if we communicated clearly.

"I need to solve this, Hattie. I need to know you're safe and that we can finally be together without having to look over our shoulders or worry that some creep is out there watching and waiting until the perfect moment to hurt you or take you from me."

Whimpering, she clung to me. My chest tightened at the mixture of fear and devotion radiating from her. With a knuckle under her chin, I tilted her face up. Brushing my thumb along her lower lip, I searched her expression for an indication that she truly understood.

"You really mean that? Like this is...I mean we're..." Her nose scrunched in the cutest way.

I rested a hand on her knee and pressed a quick kiss on the tip of her nose. "Yes, Hattie. I really mean that. This isn't something casual, at least not for me."

"Me either." She shook her head and shifted in my lap, the move causing her thigh to brush against my already hard as fuck cock.

I groaned, desperate to be inside her. But I needed to tell her one more truth, and I hoped like hell it wouldn't change things for her. "But there will be times like this, where I spend hours at the station, desperate to solve a case. It becomes an obsession, almost. It's been a point of contention in most of my relationships. Even before I took the detective exam, I picked up extra shifts, worked toward my next rank, or volunteered to help Aiden and his old partner before he retired. I promise to try harder to be mindful of that and to clue you in. But a cop's life is not an easy life—"

She placed a finger on my lips. "I'm sorry I jumped to conclusions. But I promise, as long as you tell me we're good and you're just busy, I can handle that. Your job is important. I'd never expect you to put my happiness above the safety of another person."

Heart clenching, I nodded. "Do you mind if I tell Rhett about us before we tell anyone else? I feel like he needs to hear it from me first."

She chuckled. "Remind him that I have a mean right hook and warn him that he'll be reacquainted with it if he even thinks about laying a finger on you."

Shit. The mention of a punch was a harsh reminder of how Rhett hit Jackson when he found out he was sleeping with Ashley. I cringed. Hopefully my conversation with him would go more smoothly. But if it didn't, I'd stand my ground and tell him nothing was changing.

I was in love with his sister.

Chapter Twenty-Seven

HATTIE

I SHIFTED on his lap again, and when he groaned, I couldn't help but smirk. I wanted so badly to position myself over him and rub shamelessly against his hard length. But I'd never been good at taking the lead. I'd always had trouble keeping my thoughts from taking over.

"Straddle me, Hattie," he commanded. "Need to feel you."

Though I'd hated it in the beginning, now Dylan's bossiness worked for me. I'd never been with someone like him, but knowing he was leading and I had to follow directions helped me stay in the moment. He squeezed my leg and then helped me guide myself to sit back on his lap with my legs on either side of him. Then he ran his hands up and under my sleep shorts and gripped my ass tightly, using his hold to move me back and forth along his hard shaft.

"Fuck, baby," he growled. "That feels too good."

He stopped abruptly and tossed his head back. Then, in a flurry of movement, he picked me up and laid me on the sofa. His fingers went to the waistband of my shorts, and before I could blink, he had them and my panties off and was throwing them across the room.

My pulse quickened. God, it was incredible, knowing he was as desperate for me as I was for him. He buried his face between my legs before I even realized that was his intention.

"Dylan," I moaned, lifting my ass up.

He held my hips down as he swiped his tongue across my clit in rapid succession. But when he stopped, I looked down at him and was met with his intense stare.

"Never doubt how I feel about you."

With my teeth pressed into my bottom lip, I gave him a slight nod. He ran his tongue lightly over my sensitive flesh, and a whimper left my lips.

"You're mine," he said, looking up at me again with a smirk. "Don't ever question that."

Finally, he lowered his mouth back down and began working me over, winding me up until I was writhing and bucking into his face.

God, I was so close. It felt too good, and I was about to explode. I threaded my fingers through his hair, gripping it tightly as I matched his rhythm.

His phone rang from the kitchen, and I groaned, praying he wouldn't stop.

Like he'd read my mind, he plunged two fingers inside me, the move making me buck off the cushion.

"Need you to come, baby," he said against my pussy, his eyes focused on me as he continued working his fingers in and out.

I threw my head back, trying to ignore his phone. "Do you need to get that?" I gasped. Was I losing my mind? Because I would die if he stopped.

"Not until after my girl screams my name." He covered my clit with his mouth and sucked as he hit my G-spot with his fingers.

Pleasure ripped through me, pulling a scream from my lungs, just like he'd predicted. I held him tightly to my core, riding out each wave that cascaded over me.

He smirked and brushed his mouth over the sensitive skin on the inside of my thigh. "Don't move. I'm not done with you yet."

God, I hoped not. As he hopped up, his eyes bright, he wiped his mouth and headed into the kitchen.

"Yeah, she's here," Dylan said as he moved back into the living room, holding his phone. "It's Rhett. He said he's tried your phone a couple of times."

What could he possibly need? He gave me the day off, for Christ's sake.

"It's upstairs." I sat up and snagged my shorts off the floor. I couldn't speak to my brother while I was naked from the waist down. Once I was dressed again, I took the phone from Dylan. "What do you need?" I asked my brother, who apparently had impeccable timing.

"Tina went into labor this morning."

I stared wide-eyed at Dylan. "Where are the kids?"

"At Mom and Dad's."

I nodded. "Okay. Do they need anything right now?"

"Yeah." He paused, then his voice was muffled, like he'd pulled the phone away from his mouth and was talking to someone. A moment later, he spoke into the phone again. "Bella and Ashley aren't here."

They were in Asheville, putting in our quarterly dessert order at the bakery, but what did that have to do with Tina being in labor?

"What do Tina and Kyle need?" I should have known it would be better to be direct with Rhett the first time.

"Since you're just around the corner, can you swing by and turn off the Crock-pot?"

"Like now?" Weren't those things supposed to run all day? Seemed like a waste to not let it finish cooking first.

"Yeah." A frustrated sigh came through the phone.

"Why?" Maybe they'd had it cooking overnight and had forgotten to turn it off.

"No idea."

I huffed out a breath. "Did you not ask?"

"Kyle was stressing about some outrageous scenario where, if a Crock-pot was left on while no one was home, the house could burn down."

Hmm. That actually sounded familiar.... Bella mentioned watching a TV show where something like that happened. I'd thought it was the most ludicrous thing I'd ever heard. I'd never understand why Kyle stressed about the most far-fetched things. Although I hadn't believed that I had a stalker two weeks ago, so maybe stressing about possible worst-case scenarios wouldn't be the worst thing.

"I assumed the priority was to tell him I'd take care of it so that he'll stop worrying."

By pawning it off on me? I shook my head. Whatever. "Okay. How am I getting in?"

"Kyle says Dylan has a spare."

I glanced up at Dylan. "You have a spare key to Kyle and Tina's?"

It was funny, really, that my brother trusted Dylan with a spare key over his siblings.

"Yeah." He nodded. "He gave it to me when you all went to the beach last summer."

Once I'd ended the call, I filled Dylan in. I really wanted to dive back into what we'd been doing when the phone rang, but before I could suggest it, he pulled me in for a hug and pressed his lips to my forehead.

"Why don't you get your shower, and then I'll drive you over?"

I cinched my hands behind his back and tilted my chin up so I could look at him.

As if he could read my thoughts, he added, "We can finish what we started later. I need to call Aiden back too. He says it's not urgent, but he wanted to fill me in on something Seabass found."

"Okay."

"Sounds like we got this guy on camera fleeing the back of The Dock on Wednesday night." He searched my face, his brow furrowed. "But that might mean we're going to spend all weekend gathering more footage to track him."

Nodding, I gave him a reassuring smile. "I know. If you want, I can bring lunch by the station."

His body relaxed. "That'll be great. I'll make sure Chris knows."

Eventually, I'd have to let him go, but I held on a little longer, not ready for our moment together to end.

Chapter Twenty-Eight

DYLAN

Fuck, I wasn't sure I had any patience left. I'd barely seen my girl all weekend. Apart from waking up in each other's arms and going to bed like that too, we'd only spent time together when she stopped by to drop off lunch on both Saturday and Sunday and I stepped away to chat with her for a few minutes.

"There." Seabass pointed to my computer monitor, where we had video footage from the gas station camera pulled up.

A man wearing a baseball cap disappeared around the back

of the gas station, his head lowered, making it impossible to see his face.

"What about a camera behind the building?" he asked.

I shook my head. "No, they've only got them at the front and one inside."

He grunted. The lack of cameras in town, even residences, in Half Moon Lake had been a point of contention for him. All weekend, we'd tracked this guy using the recordings we could find, starting with The Dock. Of course, we still didn't have a name or much of a description for our suspect, but we were one step closer.

My gut was saying this guy was Hattie's stalker.

"How do we know it's the same guy from the footage at The Dock?" Aiden leaned forward to examine the blurry image that was now paused on my screen.

On Friday, when I'd sent Seabass to the station, Aiden had shown him what we'd pulled from the marina side of The Dock and the footage Randy had sent us from the camera mounted at the back of his shop. He'd had problems with vandalism last year and had installed one to watch the fenced lot where he kept customer cars overnight.

"Let me show you." Seabass clicked a few files and pulled up four images. "Here's the one of him running toward the woods near The Dock." He minimized that photo and dipped his chin. "This one is behind Randy's shop." A third image. "This one is out front of the florist." Then there was one final still shot. "This one from the gas station. All the same hoodie and baseball cap."

We'd collected as much footage from the businesses along Main Street as we could, tracking this guy until he disappeared down the road leading out of town. The gas station where the first burner was purchased was the only establishment on that road for at least five miles.

"Okay. I'm going to pull a few guys to comb the area

around the gas station." Aiden squinted at the screen. "Looks like he pulls a plastic bag from the pouch of his hoodie as he disappears around the corner."

I nodded, noticing that as well. But it had been five days since that night at The Dock. I doubted we'd find anything.

"You and I can go talk with the gas station manager." Aiden headed toward our captain's office, probably to see who we could pull to help us out. "Maybe the attendant working that night will recognize this asshole," he said over his shoulder.

My phone vibrated in my pocket, and I pulled it out.

Hattie: What time should I bring lunch over?

I GLANCED AT MY WATCH. Almost eleven o'clock already? Damn.

Me: We're heading out for a bit. Why don't I text you when we're on our way back?

Hattie: Okay

I TUCKED MY PHONE AWAY, and when I looked up, Seabass was watching me, one brow cocked.

He shook his head. "Great, another one who can't keep it in his pants."

Anger sizzling in my veins, I glared at him.

"Just stating the obvious." He smirked, raising his hands in mock surrender. "I asked Nick to send a few guys down to help with protection when Hattie visits her new niece."

"Thanks." I huffed. "Although I think Kyle is being over-the-top."

She had plenty of protection between Ethan, Seabass, and

me, but Kyle wasn't satisfied, and our station was small. We didn't have the manpower to humor him.

"Yeah, maybe. But I get it. He wants to make sure his family is safe."

Yeah, I supposed I did too. So far, the stalker had stayed in the shadows, but that could change in the blink of an eye.

The whole way to the gas station, all I could think about was what it would be like if I could go home tonight and tell Hattie we got him.

The jolt of excitement was followed by dread, because once we caught the stalker, Hattie would move back to her apartment. I wanted her safe, and I was desperate to get this guy behind bars, but the thought of her being anywhere but in my house with me sat like lead in my gut.

After talking with the gas station manager and the attendant who was on shift that night, we'd gotten no new information. I drove back to the station with my hands clenched tight around the wheel. Why couldn't we catch a single break in this damn case? Who was this guy? A ghost?

Neither the manager nor the attendant recognized him. The best shot we had of the fucker showed little more than a baseball cap, one ear, and his jaw. The only thing we knew was that he was a white male.

We did find a plastic bag of spray paint behind the dumpster out back, but I had little hope that we'd pull prints from any of the items. If he was smart enough to use stolen tags, it was safe to assume that he'd worn gloves. Though maybe he wasn't all that smart, since he didn't bother to ensure the bag of spray paint actually landed in the dumpster rather than falling behind it.

The silver lining here was that I had another night with my girl. Did that make me a selfish bastard? Maybe. But being with her was everything I never knew I'd been missing.

Chapter Twenty-Nine

HATTIE

Tuesday 9:22 p.m.
All the single ladies

Savannah: How's it going with the sexy detective, Hattie? Please tell us he's good in bed.

Me: 😊

Sarah: Tina had A LOT to say on this topic when I stopped by to visit.

Savannah: I'm so here for this. Spill the tea.

Sarah: I feel like the mom of the group when you use slang like that.

Brittney: Let's go back to what Tina had to say.

Me: Don't you all have better things to do than gossip about my sex life?

Rachel: Did you just confirm that you have a sex life for us to gossip about?

Savannah: I think she did.

Brittney: WHAT DID TINA SAY?

Sarah: oh, lol.

Sarah: Tina said she thought it was ridiculous how many guys Dylan had gathered around the house today while Hattie visited. Until, that is, she saw the way he was looking at our Hattie the whole time. Then it all made sense.

Sarah: She definitely thinks they're banging, plus more.

Savannah: I knew it!

Brittney: Does Rhett know yet? Because Jackson saw you two at The Dock last week, and he isn't buying the whole "it's only for show to lure the stalker out" business.

Kelly: GIF of someone eating popcorn

Rachel: GIF asking anyone there

Cece: GIF of crickets chirping

Savannah: GIF of skeleton tapping fingers

Brittney: Titanic GIF of Rose saying it's been 84 years

Savannah: I'll get it out of her tomorrow at work.

Me: You guys are ridiculous. But fine. Yes, the sex is amazing. Beyond amazing. He is perfect. I'm hanging out with Ashley and Bella tomorrow night while Dylan hangs with Rhett and Jackson. He mentioned telling him then, so please keep this to yourselves.

Rachel: I'm shook. Totally didn't think she'd tell us.

Savannah: Wait, why wasn't I invited to hang out tomorrow night? Bitches.

Brittney: That's your takeaway?

Savannah: Yup. I already knew they were banging.

Me: Talk to Ashley. She's the one who invited us over.

Rachel: Another one bites the dust. Soon we're going to have to change our thread's name.

Savannah: I'm never settling down, so I'll be the only single lady left.

Rachel. At this point, I might settle for being a crazy cat lady.

Me: Turning off my notifications and climbing into bed with my sexy detective. Good night, bitches.

Chapter Thirty

"We should stop at the gas station and grab a six-pack," Dylan said as he rested his hand on my thigh.

The last two days had been a strange combination of perfect and difficult. Yesterday Dylan had moved heaven and earth so I could visit with Kyle, Tina, and the kids. Including my adorable new niece, Emma.

"Jackson probably has beer." I glanced over at him, watching the way the lights from the road illuminated his face in the darkened car every few seconds.

Although he was working an absurd number of hours to solve this case, we'd made sure to communicate clearly and often, and things had been great. I missed him terribly, but I would never hold that against him.

And now it felt like we were going on a double date, or maybe a triple date? Although technically it wasn't, since we hadn't gone public yet. Dylan hoped he could rectify that tonight, starting with telling Rhett. With any luck, having Jackson there as well would help keep Rhett from being unreasonable.

He raised an eyebrow at me. "He'll have liquor or craft beer. He never has light beer."

He was probably right. My brother-in-law had expensive tastes, and I doubted he would have cheap light beer on hand.

Inside the gas station, I caught sight of the young guy working behind the counter and cringed. When he sent me the smarmy smile he always did, I turned away quickly, breaking eye contact. Dylan rubbed my shoulder as he picked out his beer and made sure I didn't want anything.

After he paid, we made our way back out to the parking lot.

"Ugh, that guy always creeps me out." I glanced back to the window where the guy was watching us.

Dylan frowned and peered back at the store. "The guy behind the counter?"

I nodded. "Yeah."

"Why?"

"I don't know." I lifted my shoulders slightly. "He always comes across as kinda slimy."

He raised one eyebrow. "And you're just now telling me this?"

I tilted my head, my stomach flipping at the disappointment in his tone. "Um, yeah."

He sighed and pulled at the back of his neck. "You probably should have mentioned him when we came up with that list of people worth looking into."

He was right, but honestly, I had trouble considering that anyone around our tiny town would actually want to stalk me. Even this guy. Why would I? Flirting, even if it came across as sleazy, didn't mean he was capable of stalking someone.

"I only come here once in a while, so I didn't even think about him until just now."

Dylan's face hardened, his focus fixed on something outside the windshield. I followed his gaze, noting a dark-colored four-door car in one of the spaces to the far left of the lot.

"He could be our guy," Dylan mumbled, his expression hyper focused on the car. After a moment, he shook his head and forced his attention back to me. "I want to head into the station and look into this."

My stomach flipped as I looked back toward the store to see the guy still watching us. "I doubt it's him."

"Maybe not. But a car just like that one"—he nodded in that direction—"followed you that night. So my gut is telling me to look into this." His gaze softened as he reached out and took my hand. The reassurance brushed away the unease. "You okay if I drop you off at Ashley's? I'll have Seabass meet us there to keep an eye out and bring you back home."

Disappointment had my shoulders dropping. But this was his job, and I'd just told him I could handle it. Not only that, but I was anxious for this whole debacle to be over so we could move on with our lives.

"Yeah," I breathed, giving his hand a squeeze. "That's fine."

He studied me for a minute, his lips turned down. "You sure?"

If I really wanted him to, he'd put it off until morning. I could tell by the questions swirling in his eyes. But I knew his mind was already racing, already focused solely on the man inside the store. He wouldn't rest until he could look into it.

"Yes. I'm sure. I want you to catch this guy too."

With a squeeze of my hand, he angled over the center console and brushed his lips against mine. After he called Seabass to update him, we were on our way to Ashley's.

Part of me considered telling him I'd rather skip out on tonight and beg him to let me hang out at the station with him, but Ashley had specifically asked if Bella and I could come by. I had a feeling she needed advice, or maybe she had news to tell us.

Could she be pregnant?

I wasn't sure, since last year, when Tina announced that she was pregnant, Ashley had mentioned that she and Jackson had talked about adopting or fostering if they wanted another child.

Seabass was waiting out front when we pulled up, and as we approached him, he sent me a smile.

"Looks like I'm your date tonight," he said with a wink.

Dylan growled, and I held back a chuckle. Though I'd be lying if I said I didn't love that he was jealous.

"You're so easy to mess with." Seabass barked a laugh.

I ran my hand down Dylan's arm, garnering his attention.

His face relaxed as he studied me. After a silent moment, he wrapped his arm around my shoulders, pulling me into his side.

"I'll see you at home later," he said, his lips ghosting over my temple.

With a nod, I reluctantly untangled from his hold and walked up to Ashley's door with Seabass following behind me.

I tried to stay in the moment while Ashley, Bella, and I hung out. But my thoughts kept drifting to Dylan.

"That's amazing." Bella gave Ashley an excited hug. "So happy for you guys."

Shit. I blinked back to the moment. "Wait, you guys were approved?"

She had been explaining that they'd put in an application to foster another child, possibly more, but I guessed I'd missed the part where she told us that they'd been approved.

"Yeah, I just said that." Ashley tilted her head, looking me over with a frown.

"Sorry, I must have zoned out." I stood and gave her a quick hug. "Congratulations."

Bella smirked at me, and the look the two of them shared had me rolling my eyes. Bella wasn't our biological sister, but she'd been close to all of us since we were kids, so sometimes it felt like she was. Because of that, I'd seen these two share looks like this since I was old enough to remember.

"Alright. Out with it."

Ashley shifted on her large leather sofa and peeked back at the guys, who were standing around the kitchen.

"You and Dylan…"

I pressed my lips together, considering how much I should tell them. I didn't want either of them to have to lie to their husbands.

"Maybe I should plead the fifth until he has a chance to talk to Rhett."

Ashley turned to Bella and whispered, "I knew it."

Bella shook her head. "Hopefully Dylan has better luck than Jackson did."

"It'll be fine," I confirmed. "There's no drama or anything. He just needs to find time to talk to him."

It would be a simple conversation, and hopefully Dylan was closing in on my stalker and we could put all of this behind us and be together soon.

Like for real.

Chapter Thirty-One

DYLAN

"Have you connected him to the car yet?" Aiden stepped into the small open space that housed our desks.

After dropping Hattie off, I called him and told him about the man at the gas station. He was just as ready as I was to be done with this case, so he offered to come in and comb through the blue lady orchid buyers.

I nodded at the printer that sat on a table against the far wall. "Yeah, just printed the registration."

The first thing I'd done when I got back to the station

tonight was look up the black Toyota Corolla that was sitting in the gas station lot. It came back as registered to Brian Taylor, who, I confirmed with the gas station manager, was the young guy behind the counter tonight.

Aiden grabbed the paper off the printer. "The tag doesn't match the one you saw the night Hattie was followed, but that doesn't mean anything."

"Yeah, you know how that goes. He's probably switching them out."

"Okay. Let's see if we can find a connection with the orchids."

We spent the next two hours looking through the list of buyers from the blue lady supplier and sorting through the ridiculous number of Brian Taylors on the list. Several were in the US, but none had lived in North Carolina at the time they'd ordered the flowers or seeds.

I put my elbows up on my desk and pressed the heels of my hands against my tired eyes.

When Aiden's chair scratched along the floor, I looked over at him.

He stood and stretched, arching his back. "We've been at this for two hours. We're both exhausted, and my wife is pissed that I've been putting in so many hours this week."

I knew where he was going, and he was right. Tomorrow was a new day, and we'd have Seabass to help us comb through and research each of the Brian Taylors with the hope that we could connect one to the man at the gas station. A quick look into his previous residences showed he only had two—one in South Carolina a year ago and now here—so it shouldn't take too long to confirm or cross him off the list. After finding the spray paint stuff behind the gas station and determining that the first burner phone had been purchased there—not to mention the guy owned the same type of car that had followed Hattie—it was hard not to get my hopes up that we'd found our guy. Even so, I needed concrete evidence. There was no way I'd bring this guy in without hard proof to make it an open and shut case.

My phone vibrated on my desk, so I snagged it and unlocked the screen.

> **Hattie:** On our way home. Should I wait up for you?

> **Me:** Yes. Leaving the station now.

> **Hattie:** Find anything?

> **Me:** Nothing concrete yet.

> **Hattie:** You guys will get him. I can feel it. This will be over soon.

I REALLY FUCKING HOPED that was the case.

With a heavy exhale, I stood and nodded at Aiden. "You're right. It's late. We can pick it back up tomorrow."

I was utterly exhausted by the time I steered my car toward home, but that didn't stop me from imagining what I'd do the moment I climbed into bed with Hattie.

Would she be waiting for me naked?

The moment I stepped into my bedroom and heard the shower running, excitement zipped up my spine.

Fuck yes. Hattie, wet and soapy and moaning as I plowed into her, would be even better than what I'd been envisioning.

I stepped into the open doorway of the master bathroom, disrupting the steam fogging the tiled space. Behind the foggy glass of the shower, she stood under the showerhead, the water cascading down her back, naked and looking fucking gorgeous.

I stripped down, and with one hand braced on the tile wall

and the other one on the half pane of glass, I stood mesmerized by this beautiful woman. As I drank her in, noting her breasts, her trim waist, those hips, and her round, full ass, my dick jumped.

"Hattie," I groaned.

She peered over her shoulder and gave me a once-over, her lip pulled between her teeth. "About time."

"You were waiting for me?" I moved toward her, slowly backing her into the wall, like an animal hungry for its next meal. I molded my mouth to hers, our tongues tangling with desperation until we were both breathless.

"I need you." Hands braced on the wall on either side of her head, I lowered my forehead to her. Jesus, I wanted to make this good for her. But a need like I'd never felt before consumed me. I wanted to feel her pulsing around me.

Moaning, she ran her hands up my stomach and over my chest. "Take me, Dylan."

"I want to feel you." I took her hands in mine and pinned them above her head. "With nothing between us."

Her breaths came faster again, and she nodded. "I want that too. I'm on birth control..."

"Are you sure?" I searched her face for any indication that she wasn't. "I'd never do anything to hurt you. I've been tested, and I'm good. But if you're not sure, I'll happily carry you to the bed and get a condom."

"I'm sure." She shook her head, water dripping from her lashes. "Please, Dylan. I need you."

I released her hands, and the disappointment that painted her face in response almost made me chuckle.

"You already wet for me?" I trailed my hand down over her breast, pausing to tweak her nipple. When I reached her pussy, I dragged my fingers through her wetness. "Were you thinking about all the things I would do when I got home?"

"Yes."

She arched into me with a moan as I pushed two fingers inside her, seeking out that spot that always sent her flying.

I dragged my fingers back out slowly before plunging them back in. When I was confident she was getting close, I removed my hand and stepped off to the side.

"Come here." I sat on the built-in bench that lined the far wall of the shower.

Immediately her feet moved toward me. God, how I loved that she did exactly what I asked without hesitation. The knowledge that she trusted me with her heart and her body and wasn't holding back hit me square in the chest.

"Turn around," I commanded when she stood in front of me.

She raised an eyebrow slightly but obeyed without argument.

I guided her back to straddle my lap and lined myself up to her entrance. "Sit down, baby."

Inch by torturous inch, she lowered herself. All the while, I dug my fingers into her hips and nipped at the spot between her neck and shoulder.

"Fuck, baby." I trailed my hands up over her stomach and cupped her breasts. "You feel so good like this. So tight."

I tweaked her nipples, and she arched her back in response, a moan echoing off the tile. Then I gripped her hips and moved her up and down on my hard cock.

"Right there," she panted. "Do that again."

Tipped back with my back against the cool tile, I tightened my hold on her hips and worked her over me. She was so fucking wet and warm. I wanted this to last all night. But the sensations and the view of her ass were sending me straight to the edge.

I slowed my movements and wrapped my arms around her, pulling her against me and giving myself time to enjoy this inti-

AJ RANNEY

mate moment with her. I skimmed my hands up her sides to cup her gorgeous tits, each one a perfect handful.

"Baby." I grazed her ear with my teeth, those three little words dancing on the tip of my tongue as she turned her head. I swallowed thickly as I stared deep into her eyes. Worried she might not be there yet, I held the words in. The last thing I wanted to do was ruin this moment. "Need to make you come. You feel too good like this."

She ghosted her lips over mine. "Just let me make you feel good, then."

I opened my mouth to tell her I wasn't coming without her. "I—"

"Please, let me." Need and another even more intense emotion shone in her eyes.

There was no way in hell I'd come without her, but I nodded and leaned back against the wall, praying I wouldn't die before that happened.

She braced her hands on my knees and spread her legs wider. My eyes wandered, lowering to her ass. I bit back a groan. Surely this would be the death of me. But what a way to go.

Slowly, she shifted forward and slid back down my shaft. Her hair fell in dark waves down her back, slipping over her wet skin with every move. I tangled one hand in the long strands and tugged gently, eliciting a moan.

Her movements started out slow, but before long, she was bouncing on my dick, and I was struggling to keep it together.

"Hattie." I dug the fingers of one hand into her side and tightened my hold on her hair. "Touch yourself."

Moaning, she shook her head. "I—"

"Baby, please." The pressure that had been building came to a peak as intense pleasure shot through me. "Come with me."

"I'm close." She removed one hand from my knee and slid it between her legs. "Dylan," she moaned.

"Fuck, baby." I zeroed in on where we were joined, watching as my cock disappeared between the globes of her ass. That's all it took. Fuck. With a guttural sound, I exploded, filling her up as she screamed my name over and over. The sound was like music to my ears.

I pulled her back against my chest and held her like that as we came down from the high.

"That was…"

When her words died off, I grinned. Yeah, it was indescribable. "I know."

She laid her head back against my shoulder, and I pressed my lips against her temple.

"Amazing doesn't seem like a strong enough word."

"Definitely not."

Finally, reluctantly, I encouraged her to stand and guided her into the stream of water. I lathered her loofah up and ran it along her breasts, then down over her stomach before sliding it over her pussy. She melted back into me again as I finished.

Once we were both sufficiently clean, I turned off the water and stepped out, grabbing a towel. As I dried her body and wrapped the towel around her, a feeling of utter happiness washed over me.

Quickly, though, it was tempered by the nagging sensation that I was missing something.

Chapter Thirty-Two

HATTIE

Friday 12:10 p.m.
All the single ladies

Brittney: I'm home visiting my parents this weekend while Derek is out of town. Anyone want to meet up at Mamacitas?

Savannah: Of course! I'll be there.

Sarah: I can't. Jay's on shift.

Cece: I can't. Grace has RSV.

Me: Oh no! Isn't that really bad for babies?

Cece: Not ideal, but she's doing okay for now. We just need to keep a close eye on her.

Rachel: Someone abandoned me back in Asheville, so I can't.

Brittney: You didn't want to miss trivia night because you're crushing on the host. I did ask if you wanted to come with me for the weekend.

Rachel: Yeah, yeah. He's hot, what can I say?

Kelly: Not this time. I'm working late trying to crack our newest formula at Hill Water.

Me: I'm a maybe. Dylan didn't like the idea of Mamacitas last time, so he'll probably say no.

Savannah: Tell Mr. Sexy Detective that I said loosen up and don't be controlling.

Me: That's not fair. He's just trying to keep me safe.

Savannah: Funny how you were more annoyed about it last time. He must be really good in bed.

Me: 🙄

Brittney: Tell him I'll pick you and Savannah up from work.

Savannah: Yeah, and I'll punch the asshole stalker in his face.

Me: 😏 I'll let you know.

Chapter Thirty-Three

DYLAN

Aiden, Seabass, and I had spent the last three hours trying to find a connection between our blue orchid buyers and the attendant at the gas station.

I had almost given up when one of the addresses stood out to me. I had seen it before, but it wasn't one of our guy's last known addresses. After a little more digging, I finally figured out the connection.

"Got him." My voice echoed loudly around the open space.

Aiden pushed his chair back and sidled up next to me. "Show me."

I pointed to my computer screen. "His mother used to live in South Carolina. He had them sent there."

He had two orders of the blue lady orchids sent there, actually. One a few years ago and another one not long before he moved to Half Moon Lake last year.

"Call the gas station manager and see if Brian is working right now. We'll pick him up and bring him in for questioning."

"On it," I said, picking up the phone.

The manager informed me that Brian was not working today but that he had switched shifts with someone and was more than willing to inquire as to why. Apparently, Brian had switched so he could attend a flower and garden show in Asheville.

Dammit. That would be our fucking luck.

This had to be our guy. But to find him in a crowd of people in a city almost an hour away would be difficult.

"I'll get in touch with my contact in Asheville," Aiden said. "See if they can offer us assistance with picking him up so we can question him."

The more help we had, the smoother this would go anyway.

"Sounds good." Honestly, we probably had enough to make an arrest, but first we needed to know whether he had an alibi for the night Hattie had been followed. "Just let me know when you're ready to roll out."

"Nope." Aiden shook his head. "You're staying here."

My gut dropped. "What?"

Like hell I was. I wanted to look this asshole in the eye and see what he had to say. So why the fuck would I stay here?

"You're too close to this." His expression was firm, all business. "You stay and watch Hattie."

I shook my head. No way would I miss the opportunity to be the one to slap the cuffs on this asshole.

"You're involved, and that can affect your ability to think rationally. Or are you going to try to tell me you're not sleeping with her?"

I locked my jaw. Fuck. I couldn't outright lie to him.

He scoffed. "That's what I thought."

My phone buzzed on my desk, displaying a text notification.

"I'll talk to the captain, and then I'll call my contact." Aiden turned and headed for Captain's office.

With a huff, I picked up my phone and opened the messages app.

> **Hattie:** Hey, the girls want to know if we could meet at Mamacitas tonight.

> **Me:** Not until we get this guy. Which I'm hoping will be in a few hours.

> **Hattie:** Really? Then we should be fine tonight, right?

> **Me:** I still don't like it. Not until we officially have him in custody.

> **Hattie.** Fine. Brittney will pick Savannah and me up from work tonight. Can we come back to your place to hang out?

> **Me:** Yeah, that's fine, but I'll pick you up.

> **Hattie:** Come on, this is ridiculous. He's not going to do anything with Savannah, Brittney, and a restaurant full of people there.

Hattie: And you just said you'll probably have him in custody by tonight. Not to mention, we know who it is. I promise that if I see the creepy gas station guy, I'll call you.

I PINCHED MY EYES CLOSED. Part of me really didn't want to give in, but she was right. So far this guy had just been a nuisance, and I was confident that Aiden would have him in custody within the next few hours.

With a sigh, I shot off another text.

Me: Fine. But only when/if we have him in custody.

Hattie: Thank you. *kissy face* You're the best boyfriend.

Me: I like that title.

Hattie: Me too

Me: But seriously, if for some reason we can't pick him up, then it's business as usual.

Hattie: Okay.

Chapter Thirty-Four

HATTIE

As my phone chimed with a text from Dylan, I smiled and tapped on the notification.

> Dylan: Aiden just texted. He has Brian, and he's getting ready to question him.

> Me: See? It all worked out Brittney just pulled up, so I'll text you when we leave.

Dylan: Okay.

I SLID my phone into my back pocket and headed out to the dining room, beyond relieved that this whole mess was finally over.

I was stopped twice by employees as I made my way through the packed restaurant. As a co-owner of the restaurant, I couldn't say no. Finally, I reached the bar, watching Savannah move back and forth quickly, pouring drinks.

"Brittney's here," I called over the noisy crowd.

Michael and Paul were sitting halfway down the bar, waving, so I gave them a friendly smile.

"I'll be another minute. Need to finish these drinks for table twelve."

"That's fine. I'm going to grab the food Ashley left for us."

When I mentioned that we were going to hang out at Dylan's again, she offered to make my favorite snack. And I was not a girl who ever turned down nachos.

"I'll meet you outside," Savannah said without looking up from the drink she was mixing.

"Okay." Once I'd made my way through the swinging double doors that led into the kitchen and through to the catering side of the restaurant, I grabbed the prepped container of grilled chicken nachos from the fridge and stepped over to the side door that led to the overflow lot.

I wasn't sure whether Brittney was out this way or parked in the front lot, but the weather was mild tonight, so I'd walk around if I didn't see her car right away. It would be a heck of a lot easier than dodging people in the crowded dining room anyway. Two servers had called out tonight, and I felt bad for leaving when I knew they were shorthanded, but I'd been here since nine a.m., and I needed a break.

As I stepped out into the side lot, I scanned the handful of cars parked close by. Most of the bar, kitchen, and catering staff would park out this way, but since the catering staff was gone, the lot was pretty empty. When I didn't see Brittney's car, I turned to head toward the front of the building.

I was startled by movement in my periphery and spun that way. With my hand pressed to my chest, I peered into the darkening lot and discovered Josh, who was using his phone's flashlight to search the ground by his car.

"Hey, Josh. Everything okay?"

"Yeah," he said, peering up at me. "I dropped my key fob, and now I can't find it."

Crap, the guy was probably too drunk to drive. I couldn't leave him here like this, whether he found his key or not.

"Here, I can help." I set the bag of nachos down, then headed toward him, tapping the flashlight icon on my phone as I went. "Two pairs of eyes are better than one."

Although it was only seven, it was already dark. We really needed to get some more lights put up out here.

"Thank you, Hattie." He turned and searched near the rear driver's side tire, while I squatted to peer under the front of the car.

"I don't see it over here," I said, pushing against my thighs to stand.

Halfway up, Josh stepped up behind me, and a chill ran down my spine. Before I could turn, he held a cloth over my mouth and cinched an arm around my middle, yanking me to my feet. I held my breath, knowing whatever was on the rag wasn't good.

My phone fell to the ground, and he kicked at it, sending is sliding away from us. I fought against his hold, trying to scream, to kick, to fight, but he was too strong. He gripped my wrist, and when I wrenched it out of his hold, I felt the beads of my bracelet press into my skin.

Finally I had to take a breath, and then everything went dark.

Chapter Thirty-Five

DYLAN

My phone vibrated on my desk, and when Savannah's name flashed on the screen, dread curled through me.

Before I could greet her, she said, "Is Hattie with you?"

"Why would she be with me?" That dread turned into a hard knot in my gut. "I thought the plan was for Brittney to pick you two up and head to my place."

"Yeah, but Hattie's not here. She walked outside a few minutes before I did, but neither of us has seen her since and she's not picking up her phone."

My heart lurched painfully, and I shot to my feet. "What?"

"I think Hattie might have gone out the side entrance, but she never made it to where Brittney was parked in the lot out front." Savannah's breath hitched. "Brittney says a car pulled out of the side lot and onto the street a minute or two before I came out."

Ice ran through my veins as I spun and headed for the door. This wasn't happening. It had to be a mistake. Aiden had Brian in custody and was getting ready to question him. She was supposed to be safe now.

"I'm on my way."

I hung up without waiting for her to respond. I almost blew past the front desk, but as I passed, I figured I'd better stop. There was no time to waste, but if I was going to find her, then I needed backup.

"Send all available patrols to The Dock," I told Chris, our desk sergeant.

"What's going on?"

"Hattie's missing."

"Fuck." His eyes widened. "You sure?"

"Heading over there now to figure out what's going on." I tapped the desk twice. "Send me some patrols."

"Will do." With that, I ran for my car. The whole drive over, I prayed this was all a misunderstanding.

When I arrived, though, and had Savannah and Brittney walk me through the several minutes before they realized Hattie was missing, it was obvious this was not a misunderstanding.

I sent Ethan and a few other patrols to scour the grounds surrounding The Dock, then retraced Hattie's steps with Savannah.

"She picked up the nachos Ashley left us from the catering kitchen, and then she must have left out this door." She pointed to the side door that was used for deliveries and staff.

"Because we found the bag of food sitting on the ground behind the door."

"Did you touch anything?"

She shook her head. "I've watched enough true crime to know better."

"How did this even happen?" Rhett boomed as he stepped into the small catering space.

"It's my fault," Savannah said, her voice shaky.

Lips pressed together, I studied her. The crop top and torn jeans, the purple streaks in her hair, and the look of devastation she was wearing. I doubted it was her fault. At the moment, I was shouldering the blame. I should never have agreed to this. Not until we were sure we'd caught the right guy. I really thought we had, but was it possible that Brian had a partner? It wouldn't be the first time in criminal history where that was the case.

"I convinced Hattie that she would be safe with us tonight and that she didn't need Dylan."

Rhett narrowed his eyes at me. "Weren't there two of you protecting her? I don't understand..."

I didn't have time for this. With Rhett still rambling on, I strode for the side door and stepped out into the darkness, pulling out my flashlight.

The light reflected off an object on the ground a few feet away. Behind me, Rhett stepped outside too. Ignoring him, I walked over to the spot where I'd seen the glint.

When my flashlight beam hit it again, I knelt and took a closer look. My heart picked up to a full-on gallop in my chest. Fear and anger swirled inside me as I confirmed that there were silver beads scattered around on the ground.

"Are you listening?" Rhett asked.

I stood and shined my light around the area, searching for anything that might help us. In the grass, about five feet away, a dim light caught my eye.

Rhett followed me as I went to check it out. "Why are you ignoring me?"

I spun on him. "Because I'm trying to do my fucking job."

He flinched in response to my tone, but I didn't give a shit. I needed to find Hattie.

"I can't do this with you right now." I turned my back on him and knelt near a phone mostly hidden in the grass. With a stick I found nearby, I flipped it over. Her lock screen lit up, and a photo of her holding baby Emma stared back at me through a cracked screen.

"Imagine if it were your sister."

I whirled on him again. Between the heart-wrenching worry and the knowledge that I had limited time to save my girl, I had no patience. "Imagine if it were Bella, because that's how I feel right now." I spat the words through gritted teeth.

"What?" His eyes went wide.

I stepped closer and glared at him. "Yeah, I'm in love with your sister. I need to find her. So let me do my job. Once she's safe, we can talk." I brushed past him, heading back to the side entrance.

I couldn't even be happy about not getting punched.

At my direction, one of the patrol officers roped off the area so it wouldn't be disturbed. Frankly, I had no time to wait for our tech to dust for fingerprints, but I should get her over here anyway.

After updating Violet, I stepped back into the dining room of the restaurant. Savannah stood by the bar.

"Anyone leave around the time Hattie did?" I asked.

Maybe one of them saw something that could help me figure out what the hell was going on. And I still needed to call Aiden. Had we brought in the wrong guy? Or were there two of them?

"Josh did," Michael said from his regular spot at the bar. "He left a few minutes before her."

I studied him, then the guy beside him, noting that the third in their trio wasn't here. "Josh? Your friend with blond hair?"

Michael nodded. "Said he had to go check on his flowers."

Heart thumping, I stepped closer. "Flowers?"

"Yeah. He's obsessed with them."

Paul turned toward me. "He has a fucking greenhouse in his backyard. It's crazy."

Obsessed and crazy were the words that stood out to me. Could Josh have taken Hattie? Was he working with Brian?

I swallowed past the lump in my throat. "What kind of flowers?"

Michael shrugged. "All kinds and colors."

I fisted my hands at my sides. They obviously weren't going to be any more helpful. "Thanks."

I headed out to my car, pulling up Aiden's number as I went. We needed to see whether Josh was on our list of buyers. I had looked into all three regulars after I'd chatted with them that first day, but Josh didn't have a car registered to his name in North Carolina and neither of the other guys owned a Toyota Corolla, so I'd moved on.

Once I was in the driver's seat with my laptop, I dialed Aiden.

"Do you have a sixth sense or something?"

"What the hell is going on?" I snapped as I pulled up the buyer list.

Luckily it was in spreadsheet form so I could sort by name.

"We just finished questioning him, but he has a pretty tight alibi for the night Hattie was followed."

"Yeah," I croaked, raking a hand through my hair violently. "Because it's not him."

I sorted the list by last name, and when Josh Calvin stared back at me, I gritted my teeth. The address listed here was in Tennessee, which was where he said he'd moved from.

"What do you mean?" Aiden asked.

"Hattie was taken. It's one of the bar regulars."

There was a clatter on the other end of the line. "Wait, how do you know?"

I updated him on the evening as I took a deeper dive into Josh's information.

"In Tennessee, there was a dark gray Toyota Corolla registered to his name, but he let it lapse." Jesus, why the fuck didn't I look deeper into the regulars? "He lives a few blocks from here."

At least he'd changed his address with the local DMV.

"Dylan," Aiden warned. "Don't do anything until we get back."

Anger blazed like fire through me. Was he fucking kidding me right now? He wanted me to sit here and twiddle my thumbs for the next hour?

"I can't wait that long."

"Dylan—"

"I'm going to get my girl back."

And I wouldn't stop until I did. She was it for me, and there was no way I could lose her. I was so fucking in love with her, and I would do anything to get her back.

A loud sigh came through the phone. "At least take backup."

"Roger that."

Chapter Thirty-Six

HATTIE

"I HEARD you talking to Ashley tonight. The timing couldn't have been better." Josh's high-pitched chuckle broke through the haze I was in.

My head throbbed, and I couldn't move my arms. Where was I?

"Finally, I had the perfect opportunity to get you away from that brainwashing detective."

Dylan.

I opened my eyes but was immediately assaulted by bright lights overhead that made my head pound harder, so I pinched them shut again quickly.

"If he hadn't stepped in and turned you against me, we would already be together."

Nausea roiled in my stomach. What the hell was he talking about? Other than being friendly and making small talk, I'd hardly ever spoken to him.

"Tonight played out even better than I'd hoped. I thought I would have to run you and your friends off the road to get to you, but then you came out the side door and made it so much easier on me."

A chill ran down my spine. Holy shit. It was strange to think this way, but god, was I thankful that he'd only grabbed me. If he'd run us off the road, he could have killed one or all of us.

"Now we can finally be together."

Bile rose in my throat. This guy was insane.

Slowly this time, I opened my eyes and surveyed my surroundings. Was I in a greenhouse? It had to be. The enclosure was lined with clear panels, and bright lights hung from the ceiling, and the space was full of all kinds of plants and flowers.

When I caught sight of a section of blue orchids across from where he had me tied to a chair, I gasped.

"They're all for you." A metal object glinted in the fluorescent lights as he waved at the flowers. Oh god. *A knife*. "Blue like your eyes."

I moved my wrists, tugging gently on the ropes. They were tied securely, so I plastered on a fake smile and nodded.

"I knew you would love them."

"They're beautiful." It was the only idea I had. If I wanted to survive, I'd have to go along with him and hope like hell he couldn't see through my façade.

"After the Titans won the Super Bowl last year and you high-fived me, I knew you were perfect. I couldn't stop thinking about how the color of your eyes were the exact shade of my beautiful blue lady orchids."

Oh god. I remembered that night. The bar had been packed, and I'd stayed to help Rhett close up. Michael, Paul, and Josh were all there. A few weeks after that, I'd learned Josh had officially moved to our town.

"Is that why you moved here?" I forced the words through my lips and swallowed thickly.

Maybe I could make him think he could trust me. That his feelings were reciprocated. If he thought I wanted to be here, he might untie my hands. I'd just have to wait for the right opportunity to make a run for it. I'd been handling my siblings all my life. Surely an unhinged stalker couldn't be much worse.

His lips curled up slightly. "Yeah. Then on that night back in November, when you said you loved my new haircut, I knew it was time."

"Time?"

"For us to finally be together."

I kept the smile on my face, refusing to let it slip. For now, I had to keep him talking and get him to trust me until I could escape or Dylan came to save me.

Because Dylan would come. He would figure it out, and he wouldn't stop until he found me. Fate had intervened so far. He was meant to be the one protecting me. He looked at puzzles and mysteries with the same intensity as when he looked at me. And I trusted he would find me.

But...

Another thought struck me, and my stomach bottomed out. What if this crazy asshole killed him?

A tear slipped from my eye and ran down my cheek.

Stay safe, Dylan. I silently sent the plea out into the universe.

I'd been so stupid, leaving the restaurant alone. God, I'd never get over it if I got him killed.

Chapter Thirty-Seven

DYLAN

I ROLLED to a stop in front of the address I'd found for Josh, and just as I climbed out, two patrol cars pulled up with their lights and sirens off.

"You two cover the front in case he tries to make a run for it." I pulled my weapon out of its holster and turned to Ethan. "You're with me."

"Yes, sir."

In a crouched position, I inched to the far corner of the house and peered into the large front windows. It was dark inside, apart from radiant light coming from the back, but all was quiet.

"Stay on my six." I whispered over my shoulder.

The greenhouse in the middle of the backyard came into view as we came around the house. The walls looked like they were made of a thick polycarbonate, and the door was ajar.

Shadows moved against the opaque panels of the structure, and faint voices carried on the air.

Crouching lower, I silently crept to the door that faced the back of the house.

"Tomorrow we'll head to Mexico. It'll be you and me forever." Josh's nasally voice sent fire coursing through my veins.

That wasn't ever going to happen. She was *mine*.

"Why Mexico?" Hattie asked.

Tension eased from my shoulders at the sound of her voice. She was okay. But I still needed to get her out of there safely.

I signaled to Ethan to stay put, then I moved to the back of the greenhouse. Josh had Hattie toward the front, so if I came in from the back, I could maybe sneak up behind him without being noticed. Slowly, I tried the handle, and when I found it unlocked, I breathed a sigh of relief.

Still in a crouched position, I moved down the aisle of plants until I was standing behind Josh and had a visual on Hattie.

She noticed me right away, but other than a slight widening of her eyes, she didn't react. *Good girl*.

"Hopefully you don't make me use this." He set a large knife on a table and picked up a syringe filled with God knew what.

Now that he'd put the knife down, it was time to draw his attention to me and away from Hattie. No way would I let him inject anything into her.

"You won't need to," I said, quickly observing the open

space around us. The aisles ended right behind me, and there was only a chair and workbench at the front.

In the space of a heartbeat, he grabbed the knife and spun to me, his eyes wild and his hair sticking up all over. "You."

"Put the knife down, Josh." I kept my gun aimed at him and took a few small steps, circling him and hoping to get in a position where I could get between him and Hattie if I needed to. Or, worst-case scenario, have a clean shot at Josh without her behind him.

"You turned her against me."

I knew better than to try to rationalize with him. I took a steadying breath and cursed my hands as the slight quiver drew my attention. I'd never had this issue before. Always in control. Always confident and steady. But then again, I'd never had so much on the line until this moment. And for the first time in my life, I was worried about making a single mistake. But I had to keep it together, so I took another deep breath in and kept my attention trained on the asshole in front of me.

"Set the knife down, and we'll talk about it."

"No." With a scowl, he shook his head and looked over at Hattie.

My heart dropped to the floor. I would do whatever it took to protect her, but the last thing I wanted to have to do was fire my weapon.

"Josh," I warned. "Don't move."

"Either I get her, or no one does." In a heartbeat, he turned toward Hattie.

No, no. no. Fear swamped me, and my vision blurred as adrenaline pumped through my veins. With my body taut with worry, I moved quickly.

Praying I wasn't too late. Praying I could save her.

HATTIE

Was this what it felt like to die? My body vibrated with fear and my head thrummed with pain. I wasn't ready to open my eyes yet, afraid of what I'd find. The last vision I had was of Josh lunging at me with a knife in his hand as I attempted to throw myself, and the chair I was still tied to, over to avoid being stabbed. But I couldn't remember anything after that.

Shuffling noises and then the sound of someone howling in pain hit my ears. Was that me? Maybe I was having an out-of-body experience.

Dylan called my name—an agonizing hitch to his voice—finally forcing me to pry my eyes open. My stomach tightened. Was he hurt?

On the ground in front of me, Josh lay on his stomach while Dylan pressed a knee to the middle of his back. Dylan held my stare, agony radiating in his eyes, as he holstered his gun and pulled Josh's arms behind his back before securing his wrists with a zip tie.

A stream of blood running down Dylan's arm caught my attention, and I gasped at the sight, my heart lodged in my throat. The cut looked deep, and blood continued to gush from it as I lay, immobile, tied to this damn chair and now, feeling utterly useless.

Dylan glanced down at the slash across his bicep and groaned. "You chose the wrong woman to fuck with."

As he shifted his weight on Josh's back, Josh howled out in pain.

"All clear."

Ethan stepped inside and headed straight toward them, wearing a cocky smile. "Well, that was easy."

Easy? He wasn't the one who'd had a psychopath with a knife lunging at him.

Dylan glared at him, then stood and let him take over. "Read him his rights and lock him in the back of a squad car."

"Sure thing, Boss." Ethan tipped his head at Dylan's arm. "You need to get that looked at. Definitely gonna need stitches."

He nodded but kept his gaze focused on me. "Yeah, it'll have to wait, though. I have more important things to do first."

Those words sank deep into my soul, making me feel seen and important to someone for the first time in a very long time.

Chapter Thirty-Eight

DYLAN

IN THREE LONG STRIDES, I was crouching in front of Hattie and lifting the chair to an upright position. She had hit her head pretty hard when she tipped herself sideways, and my first task was to make sure she wasn't bleeding. After running my hand over the side of her head and not finding blood, I relaxed.

Cupping her face with my hands, I pressed my lips to her forehead. The smell of fresh rain enveloped me, instantly soothing my frayed nerves. "You okay?"

Sniffling, she nodded, her eyes welling with tears. "Your arm."

Gently, I looped my hands around her to untie the rope securing her wrists. "It's not that deep. It'll be fine."

"I thought he was going to"—her throat moved as she swallowed—"kill me. Then I was scared he hurt you."

"I know, baby." I rested my forehead against hers as I loosened the rope. "But it's over now. And we're okay. We're both okay."

My body relaxed only slightly as I repeated those words in my head.

Draping her arms around my neck, she fell against me. For a long moment, we stayed like that, just breathing one another in. Finally, I slid my arm under her knees and picked her up, wincing and ignoring the pain.

"Dylan, your arm." Worry etched her features as she swatted at my chest. "I can walk, you know."

"I know. But you hit your head and might have a concussion, so let me carry you, okay?"

Sighing, she snuggled her face into the place where my shoulder meets my neck. "Only if you promise to let me look at your arm when we get to your car."

"Deal." I didn't set her down until I'd made it to the passenger side of my SUV. Once she was seated inside the vehicle, I held her face in my hands again, searching her face for any marks or bruises.

"Dylan." She covered my hands with hers. "I'm okay. I promise."

With a deep exhale, I angled in and brushed my lips tenderly against hers.

"Now, where's your first-aid kit?" The look she sent me told me to not even try to brush it off again.

After opening the glove box, I pulled out a small kit and set it on her lap. I bit down on my back teeth as she quietly cleaned the wound.

"Not sure if it needs stitches or not, but it looks like the bleeding is slowing." She pressed a large bandage over the cut.

"Your brother knows," I blurted out as she began taping the bandage to my arm.

Her eyes went wide.

"I told him I'm in love with his sister."

That brought a shy smile to her face. "Really?"

I nodded, though I was suddenly nervous to admit just how deep my feelings for her ran. What if this whole situation had made her realize how dangerous my job could be?

"Good." She applied tape around the last edge of the bandage and then ran a hand through my hair, her eyes shining in the dim streetlight above. "'Cause I love you too." Quickly, she pressed her lips to mine. "Now, can you take me home?"

Realization dawned on me then. She no longer needed my protection. But the thought of taking her back to her apartment didn't sit well with me. Though if that was what she needed, I would do it. I'd do anything for her.

"Yeah, of course." I searched her face, memorizing every inch of it. "I need to finish a few things up and give Aiden an update. He and Seabass should be back from Asheville any minute now. Plus." I tipped my head to the ambulance that had just pulled up. "We both need to get checked out. But after that, I can drive you back to your apartment."

Her eyes widened, and then her brows pulled together. "I'm fine going to the hospital or my apartment or your house, but I don't want to go anywhere without you."

"Then I would love nothing more than to take you back to my place after we both get checked out." My body still buzzed with adrenaline, but pure joy coursed through me too.

If I had anything to say about it, my place would become *our* home sooner rather than later.

Because I had every intention of spending the rest of my life with this woman.

Chapter Thirty-Nine

DYLAN

I CROSSED my arms and leaned back in the chair, letting my head fall back against the cold plastic and closing my eyes. My arm only needed six stitches, and thankfully they were quick about it so I could be in here with Hattie before they took her back for a CT scan.

At the sound of a throat clearing, I straightened, finding Rhett standing at the entrance to the small ER unit.

Before either of us could say anything, Hattie's sisters, along with her mom and Bella, appeared behind him. Knowing the front desk ladies, they likely let more people than typically allowed back here, but the rest of the family was probably still in the waiting room.

"Where is she?" Bella stepped up next to Rhett, scanning the room.

"She's getting a CT. Should be back in a few minutes."

"What happened?" Ashley asked with a worried frown, her blond hair pulled up into a messy bun.

I filled them all in on the details. I'd given them a quick summary through text and told them we were heading to the hospital, but I'd expected an inquisition when they arrived.

"Can we talk?" Rhett tipped his head toward the hallway. "Outside."

With a nod, I stood and followed him out of the room. This conversation could probably wait, but we might as well get it over with. And frankly it wasn't going to change anything. If he wasn't okay with me dating his sister, then I'd have to hold out hope that he would eventually come around. Because Hattie was my future.

He turned the corner and stopped just down the hall, spinning to face me.

"Look, man," I spit out quickly. "I know you're pissed—"

He held up his hand. "I'm not mad."

I cocked my head. Then what the hell were we standing here for?

"It's obvious you care about her. I saw that earlier." He ran his hand through his hair. "I just wanted to apologize for the way I acted. I didn't mean to come at you like that. I was freaking out."

"It's fine. Emotions were running high." This definitely wasn't how I saw this conversation going, but fuck, I was elated. "You're good with Hattie and me?"

He smirked. "Yeah. Couldn't ask for anyone better for her.

There are details I never, ever want to hear about." He patted my shoulder. "But I'm happy for you both."

"Thanks, man."

Back inside the small room, I immediately sought out Hattie, who was already studying me with questions in her eyes.

"Everything okay?"

I nodded and gave her a soft smile. "Yup. Everything's perfect."

There were far too many people in the room, and every one of them was asking Hattie questions about tonight's events.

When she flinched and brought a hand to her head for the second time in the last ten minutes, I addressed the room.

"Alright, guys. Hattie needs to rest. She probably has a nasty headache, and all the lights and sounds are probably making it worse." I stepped off to the side and waved toward the hall. "If you want to hang out in the waiting room, I can update you once she's spoken to the doctor."

After another round of questions and assurances that I would come out to give them an update once I had it, they were gone, and I took my seat next to Hattie's bed and entwined our hands.

"Thank you." She squeezed my hand.

I brought hers to my mouth, brushing my lips across the back. "Of course." I stood and climbed into the bed next to her, wrapping my good arm around her shoulders and guiding her to lay her head on my chest. "I'd do anything for you."

I planned to show her that every day for the rest of our lives.

Chapter Forty

DYLAN

I STOOD IN *OUR* KITCHEN, smiling over my coffee mug as Hattie devoured her bacon. It had been almost three months since Josh had abducted her, and we were both sleeping more soundly now that he'd been convicted and was behind bars. It actually didn't take much convincing to get her to move in with me. We were spending most nights here anyway, so two months in, we moved all her belongings over.

"I'm still hungry." She chuckled as she rinsed her plate.

"Probably because we worked up an appetite in the shower."

She spun and gave me a smirk, a blush creeping into her cheeks. "I'd be okay with that type of workout every day."

"I'm going to hold you to that." I tipped my head toward the middle of the island. "There are donuts left." Pushing away from the counter, I stalked toward her. "Or I can make you something."

"This is fine." She grabbed a powdered donut and took a massive bite.

Grinning, I brushed my thumb along her lower lip, wiping off the excess sugar.

Her eyes blazed in response to my touch, making my dick perk up.

I backed her up against the counter and dragged my nose up her neck, then forced myself to straighten. "If I didn't need to leave for court soon, I would take you back upstairs and spend the rest of the day inside you."

She lifted the donut to my lips, and I took a bite. As I did, I made a point to suck her finger into my mouth.

"Dylan," she moaned. She tried to squeeze her legs together, but my thigh was wedged between them.

Was it cruel that I wanted to send her off for the day all worked up?

I gripped her hips and moved her against my leg.

"I thought you had to leave," she panted.

Rotating her hips, I rubbed her clit against my thigh. "I have a minute to give my girl another orgasm."

Her responding whimper made it so damn tempting to tear her clothes off and take her right here on the tile floor. Instead, I thrust my tongue into her mouth, devouring her as I continued to bring her pleasure.

Head dropping back, she moaned, the sound loud and

drawn out, and her body shook. When she came back down from her orgasm, she melted into my arms.

"Perfect." I shifted, my cock begging to be set free.

"You sure you have to go?" She looked up, sticking her lip out, and palmed my hardness.

I pinched my eyes closed and breathed deeply, wishing I could stay. But in no world could I be late for court.

With a shake of my head, I stepped back. "I really do need to leave now." I pressed a quick kiss on her forehead. "Trust me, I wish I didn't."

Smiling, she followed me to the door. "Remember we have that thing for Brendan's birthday tonight at my mom's. If you don't get stuck at the station."

I never had to question whether my job would pose a problem anymore. Hattie went with the flow and had no problem adapting if plans changed. Just last week, she'd come to the station to have dinner with me while I pulled a long shift in order to solve a case.

"It should be fine." And though Rhett's endless complaining about both of his best friends being with his sisters was a little annoying, it was more comical than anything. We weren't allowed to mention anything even remotely related to sex, or Rhett would groan and walk away.

I gave Hattie one more kiss and headed to my car.

Next door, Logan was out. He was standing on his porch, watching his young nanny play soccer with his twin girls.

I shook my head. That situation was going to implode eventually, and when it did, it would be a mess. Not only was she almost twelve years younger than him, but she was also the younger sister of one of his good friends.

Regardless, he was looking at her the way I looked at Hattie, so this was sure to be dramatic.

But sometimes the woman a guy is meant to be with comes

to him when he least expects it. And then she'll turn his world upside down.

I glanced back at Hattie, who was watching me with a smile, and my chest constricted.

If all went well tonight, we would be setting a wedding date soon, because I couldn't imagine my life without her in it.

Epilogue

HATTIE

I SMILED as I surveyed our friends and family. They were scattered around the back patio of The Dock, where we were hosting our rehearsal dinner. It still amazed me that our little group of friends and family had added so many more kids in the last year. Maybe there really was something in the water last spring, because Bella, Brittney, and Sarah all had infants close in age.

Dylan stepped up next to me and handed me a glass of wine. "The rehearsal went well, don't you think?"

I raised an eyebrow at him. "Sure, if you don't count the shitshow Savannah caused."

Leave it to her to show up at my wedding rehearsal with a date and cause an uproar.

"Eh." Dylan lifted a shoulder and let it drop. "I don't think she had a clue Kyle would respond like that. You two were so young when his best friend's sister drowned, weren't you?"

"Yeah. I think I was seven, so that would have made Savannah five." Honestly neither Savannah nor I remember much of what happened, but obviously it had something to do with the guy Savannah brought as her date.

With his lips pressed to my temple, he pulled me into his side. "Don't let it get to you. They'll work it out."

I hoped so. As much as my family exhausted me most days, I couldn't handle it if any of them were upset tomorrow.

"At least Rhett seems okay with it."

A chuckle slipped from Dylan's lips. "I think he's just happy she didn't end up with one of his friends."

I rolled my eyes. "Not sure he has any left. If he did, Savannah totally would have dated one of his friends just to annoy him."

"Probably." His smirk morphed into a full smile.

I followed his gaze, finding Rhett holding Luna in the crook of his arm.

I couldn't wait until we had one of our own. Dylan would be an amazing dad. It wouldn't always be easy, but we had a pretty good handle on being partners and lovers. I had no doubts that we could handle being co-parents too.

Laughter erupted from the table where our parents were sitting, snagging my attention.

I shook my head. "Those four are trouble, you know that?"

He huffed a laugh. "Yeah. My parents are talking about selling their house and moving here."

Warmth bloomed in my chest. "Really?"

"Yup. They've been telling me that for years. Every time they visit. I think once we tell them they're going to be grandparents, they'll take the leap."

I glanced up at him as my mouth fell open. "You know it could take some time, right? It might not happen right away."

"I know." He kissed the top of my head. "But you know I like a challenge, so I plan to try as often as you'll let me."

My core throbbed just thinking about being with him. "Think anyone would miss us if we left now?"

He barked out a laugh and scanned our surroundings. With a hand to the small of my back, he took a step forward, urging me along. "Yes. Let's do a few more rounds, and then maybe we can leave."

"Fine." I stuck my bottom lip out in a pout. "I guess you're right."

By this time tomorrow, I would officially be his wife, and I couldn't wait to call him my husband.

More By A J Ranney

Half Moon Lake Series:

Always Yours (book 1)

Wishing to be Yours (book 1.5)

Impossibly Yours (book 2)

Imperfectly Yours (book 3)

Bravely Yours (book 3.5)

Recklessly Yours (book 4)

Half Moon Lake Heroes: The Red Line

Bravely Yours (book 0.5)

Playing with Fire

Out of the Fire

The Line of Fire (coming fall of 2025)

Calling a Cease Fire (coming 2026)

WRITING AS GRACIE YORK

Goldilocks and the Grumpy Bear

Tumbling Head Over Heels

Along Came The Girl

Peter Pumpkined Out

Back Together Again

Ghost Shoes

Follow Me

Come be apart of my Facebook Group.
AJ's Book Nook

Find me on social media:
Instagram.com/a.j.ranney
Facebook.com/ajranney19
tiktok.com/@ajranney3
Goodreads.com/AJ Ranney
http://www.ajranney.com

Note from the Author

Dear Reader,

THANK YOU for reading *Recklessly Yours*. Romantic Suspense has been a favorite genre of mine and I was excited to finally get to write one! Hattie and Dylan were so much fun to write because she drives him nuts and that reminds me a bit of my own relationship with my husband.

Next I'm working on a quick novella about a reformed playboy and his employee Angie Mitchell before giving you Logan's story. Do you think you know who his young nanny is going to be? I give you a hint in this book as well as at the end of Bravely Yours! From there you'll get all the guys at the Half Moon Lake Fire Department!

I appreciate each and every one of you. It's only because people like you read our books that authors like me get to publish them.

Check out my website for bonus content and stay up to date with latest releases.

Love,
AJ Ranney
www.ajranney.com

Acknowledgments

Like always, I need to thank my husband first. He has been one of my biggest cheerleaders, is always willing to listen to what I write, and has done bedtime with the kids more times than I probably realize. I appreciate your eagerness to help me when I'm stuck and your willingness to let me read to you.

And then to my kids, who are always curious about what Mommy is writing. And yes, you still need to wait until you're eighteen to read them. But by then I doubt you'd want to!

Jenn, I know you're sick of my stories by the time we get to this part! Regardless, thank you for dealing with my constant *how do I fix this?* questions and talking me down every time I'm ready to burn everything I write. You're always willing to read and edit multiple times, hold my hand when I need it, and tell me to just do it when I need that too. But above everything you've done, your friendship has meant the world to me.

A HUGE thank you to my author friends who have supported me in so many ways, whether through encouragement or reading my stuff: Annie Charme, Kat Long, Jenni Bara, Brittanee Nicole, Daphne Elliot, Kristin Lee, Amanda Zook, Alexandra Hale and many more!

Also to all my beta readers: thank you for always willing to read and give feedback! You definitely helped make Hattie's story so much better with all your feedback. Couldn't have done it without you!

Amy, thank you for being patient as I struggled time and time again. For helping me with Tiktok, graphics, getting organized and just being an amazing friend!

Beth, thank you for being so flexible, your edits, and the millions of questions, hand holding, and messages.

Michelle, a HUGE thank you goes out to you. Every comment you left that made me stop and think, even when I wanted to push back. Your guidance really helped shape and mold this book. Thank you for always willing to answer questions or help me talk something out!

Holly, as always, thank you for being my sister, even if not by blood—and to my mom and mother-in-law: You have been so supportive throughout every step of this crazy journey!

And finally, thank you to the rest of my friends and family who have helped or supported me. I used to think it took a village to raise little humans, and that still holds true, but it also takes a village to write and publish a book!

About the Author

A.J. Ranney lives in Maryland with her ever-growing zoo, including two kids, two cats, an attention-loving dog, a bunny, a cricket-eating lizard, and her lovable, well-meaning husband. She likes to leave the chaos of her real world behind and lose herself in a steamy romance novel. Her passion for reading romance prompted her writing journey, leading her to create relatable happily ever afters that come from her own dreams and experiences.

She loves coffee, sushi, wine, and her family. Not necessarily in that order. Her inner peace comes from the water, always relating to her zodiac sign, the Pisces. It's no wonder the small town she created in her stories is situated on a lake.